"There's another truck behind us. Don't turn around."

"How many in the cab?" Madison asked, sticking the 9mm in the back of her jeans.

"One," he answered. "Maybe some in the back also, but I cannot see." He shouted out his window to the truck blocking the road. "You broken down? Need some help?" He whispered for Madison to stay in the car, then opened the driver's door and stepped out.

Two figures emerged from the front truck, one male, one female, AK-47's pointed at Anthony. Madison heard a door slam behind her and saw in her side mirror a man climb out of the cab of the second truck.

Anthony had his hands in the air. He was smiling and shuffling, trying to make jokes. Madison heard him say he had been hired to show her the countryside, that he made his living off rich women.

Then she heard the unmistakable sound of a rifle click into firing position next to her. She turned her head slowly and saw the AK pointed at her temple.

THE SPY IN QUESTION

A Madison McGuire Espionage Thriller

AMANDA KYLE WILLIAMS

The Naiad Press, Inc.
1993

Printed in the United States of America on acid-free paper
First Edition

Edited by Katherine V. Forrest
Cover design by Pat Tong and Bonnie Liss
    (Phoenix Graphics)
Typeset by Sandi Stancil

Library of Congress Cataloging-in-Publication Data

Williams, Amanda Kyle, 1957–
    The spy in question : a Madison McGuire espionage thriller /
by Amanda Kyle Williams.
        p.   cm.
    ISBN 1-56280-037-X : $9.95
    I. Title.
PS3573.I447425S65   1993
813'.54—dc20

                                                        92-41465
                                                        CIP

For Julie

How bravely we sacrifice others
for flag and country

About the Author

Amanda Kyle Williams was born in August of 1957 and spent her formative years near Boulder, Colorado. At the age of sixteen, she left high school for a full-time job. By the age of twenty-eight, she was vice-president of a sizeable textile manufacturing company.

At thirty, she walked away from corporate America and began work on the first espionage-action thriller to feature a lesbian agent. She now resides in Marietta, Georgia with her partner Julie and their ever-growing family of cats.

Amanda Kyle Williams is also the author of *Club Twelve, The Providence File,* and *A Singular Spy.*

WORKS BY AMANDA KYLE WILLIAMS

CLUB TWELVE
THE PROVIDENCE FILE
A SINGULAR SPY
THE SPY IN QUESTION

PROLOGUE

It was a rare clear evening in the City of Kings, a city where Andean culture meets Spanish tradition with stunning results, where one can see the astounding contrast that is Peru — the jagged Andes thrusting snow-capped glaciers into white clouds, the spectacular dunes of one of the world's driest deserts, the vast Pacific breaking hard against sandy beaches.

And there is another Peru. Here sidewalk vendors jam Lima's back streets — a legion of impoverished *ambulantes*, drifting, jobless, homeless except for ramshackle hovels of sand and stone and cardboard. Here an average of six people die every day in political violence. Here some seven million nearly burst Peru's capital city at its seams. And tonight . . . Tonight the lights had been turned off.

Jay Marek, the Central Intelligence Agency's Lima Station Chief was in his private office at the time — a dreary grey room with one window and a radiator that groaned at the slightest demand. The group of offices leased by the Agency was located on the third floor of an office building that should have died of old age years ago. For cover, the stenciled sign on the door of the outer office read, *Fredrich Internacional,* and advertised alarm system installation.

Marek, like most people who have spent their lives traveling and suddenly find themselves behind a desk, had not quite learned to manage his paperwork. It was heaped on the desk top, hours' worth, perhaps days' worth, stained by his coffee mug and piled up to be locked in the safe later. There were notes in his own handwriting, mostly indecipherable even to Marek himself. A half-smoked cigar lay in the ashtray, much to the distress of Fernando who was nicknamed the housekeeper, a fanatically neat *mestizo* from the Andean highlands.

A muscular man with soft brown eyes and reddish hair, Fernando occupied a separate office tonight. He also happened to be the most effective killer employed by the Company in Peru. He had dutifully attended the Lima office for two years now and had seen two men like Marek pass through it, watched them try to rebuild the network they had inherited — a network that was reeling, like Peru

2

itself, from the recent upsurge of guerrilla attacks and too little outside financial help.

Marek had waited two weeks for a wire from Finance okaying a simple two-hundred-dollar payment to a local informant. No wonder he couldn't get reliable Intelligence. Half of his agents in the field had disappeared or been bought off, most of his couriers had found safer and more profitable ways to supplement their incomes, and his informants, what was left of them, brave souls that they were, operated now simply out of a love for Peru and fear of the Maoist guerrilla groups that threatened to destroy their beloved country while promising to save it.

The network had crumbled long before Marek's arrival, and he was allocated no resources to piece it back together. The terrorists were winning the war, and no one, certainly not the old field man, and maybe not even Langley itself, had been able to convince Washington that Peru was worth saving.

"Twenty-six armed guerrillas will attack the power station at eight-thirty," an anonymous voice reported in Spanish. The night duty officer had logged the call in at exactly eight twenty-eight and buzzed Marek, who picked up the phone and was told, "Ten electrical towers will be attacked and thirty bombs will be detonated in Lima immediately after the blackout. If you want more, meet me in front of the British Airways office at Plaza San Martin."

Marek leaned back and surveyed his fingertips calmly. "Sorry. Fredrich International doesn't do power stations. You've got the wrong number, bud."

By the time Marek replaced the receiver, the

lights were out. His electric wall clock dimmed out at eight-thirty as promised.

In the next few minutes he found the desk drawer where he kept his 9mm Beretta, yelled to the duty officer to keep the night's phone tapes, bumped his shin on an open file drawer as he looked for a flashlight, and swore something untranslatable on his way out.

Minutes later came the scream of automatic weapons from downstairs. Fernando had found the stairway door before the blast ended. He moved carefully down the dark staircase, keeping close to the wall, senses alert to any movement. At his side, a customized Czech made CZ-75 semi-automatic, the combat handgun he had relied on many times.

The unlit lobby was still, no movement, no sound. Then a footstep from behind . . .

It was a dreadful blow, seemingly out of pace with the rest of the world. The mind keeps its own time when the unthinkable happens, and a sense of unreality swept over him as he felt the first wave of pain, as his knees buckled and hit the hard tiles, as he fell and saw Jay Marek's body, so twisted it was nearly unrecognizable, saw the hand-painted message Marek's killers had left on the wall so that no one would have to wonder who should get credit for this one.

Viva El Sendero Luminoso — Long Live the Shining Path.

CHAPTER ONE

The tiny town of Helen, nestled sweetly in the lush Georgia mountains, is a charming reproduction of an old Bavarian village. But this is the American South after all, where one as likely as not would find an odd mixture of German restaurants, log cabins, Tudor-style architecture, and roadside stands with hand-painted signs advertising boiled peanuts and fresh peaches.

Tourists, anxious to escape sizzling city heat, came through Helen, spent their money, bought their souvenirs and sauerkraut and boiled peanuts and headed north for the splendor of Annaruby Falls.

But the town of Helen had sprung to life a bit early this year, on March 30th to be exact, when a stranger stopped in at Langford's General Store and asked for information on the old Stewart farm. She had come alone, the observant Mrs. Langford noticed at once, but with the hollow look of someone who had left a lot behind. Widows and drifters often wore the same expression.

Mrs. Langford had tried to persuade the woman to look at other real estate in the area. The old Stewart farm, she explained with the exaggerated gesture of one fat arm, was too rocky and too hilly. And the price! Lord, the price was ridiculously high. After all, the place had been on the market for over a year now and not a nibble. But the stranger merely smiled that sad smile and took only one look at the property before signing the papers. And all this without soliciting any further advice from the authoritative Mrs. Langford, who happened to be the local storekeeper, postmaster, notary public and source of juicy information for a good portion of White County.

"Her name is McGuire," the plump Mrs. Langford told two interested customers one day. "Claims to be a writer. She comes and picks up supplies on Fridays and back she goes up that mountain. Hardly speaks a word unless she's spoken to. I swear, I never know what to say to her. We went up there one day, Jim and me, to see how she was getting on. Well, she met us right there at the front door. Never even invited us inside. Just sat us down on the porch." She paused, deciding her words might have sounded a bit harsh, then added with a contrived smile, "She *has* done a fair amount of work on the old place though. Built a deck around the side. All by herself. A woman like that. Can you imagine?"

It took the town of Helen several weeks to adjust to the silent presence of their new neighbor — the solitary figure living up the mountain. She was quite beautiful, they all seemed to agree. A bit intense though with that unruly red hair. But a tidy English accent, and polite too. Never troubled anyone, and paid well for what help she got. So who were they to say she didn't have a right to her privacy?

And then the other woman came, and quite by chance it happened to be a Friday and quite by chance Madison McGuire, the writer, happened to be at Langford's buying her weekly supplies. And the town, egged on by Mrs. Langford of course, had since been very busy trying to assemble the pieces.

The woman had climbed out of a rented automobile in torn jeans and a cut off T-shirt. She came through the door with a map in her hands, seeking directions to a quiet resort a few miles north. The formidable Mrs. Langford had pegged her for a Rocker immediately — the dark glasses, the expensive boots, the shallow cheeks, and the prison paleness of someone who lived her life between dusk and sunrise. And only moments later, Mrs. Langford's brooding suspicions were confirmed.

She heard someone excitedly shout the woman's name, saw him run to the door and shout it again for good measure. The store filled with tourists within minutes. They came from across the street, from the store next door, from the pavement cafe, clambering around her like a flock of hungry geese. Sign this, sign that, pose for this picture or that one. And by the time Madison McGuire turned from her shopping, the crowd had done everything but mug the woman, and even then one of them had wrangled the map from her hands and run off with it like a trophy.

Mrs. Langford saw Madison turn, saw her face darken at the sight of the ambush, and watched her do something that no one in the town had been able to put together since. She pushed her way to the front of the crowd, and whispered something into the woman's ear. A moment later she had escorted the woman safely to the car and driven her away while the crowd looked on in amazement.

"Bloody feeding frenzy, wasn't it?" Madison said as she drove from the parking lot. "The name's McGuire, by the way, Madison McGuire. Does this happen often?"

The woman was sitting back with an ankle crossed over her knee, her head leaning on the headrest, and by her calm demeanor, Madison knew it was not her first quick exit. She was thin with sharp features and a mane of brown hair that reached the center of her back. Not pretty, Madison thought, if you analyzed her feature by feature, but there was something about her, a certainty, a self-assurance, a sensuality. And when she spoke, her voice was grainy and deep and Madison recognized it at once.

"It's a pain sometimes," she said easily. "Thanks for the help. I'm Dani."

Madison got her right hand free of the steering wheel long enough to shake her hand. "It's Stone isn't it? Dani Stone? Had a friend who was a big fan. I've heard your music. You're very good." She thought of Terry and remembered seeing the compact disc in the living room, remembered Terry listening to the pounding rhythm for hours while she sunned, remembered the husky voice blaring through the beach house until Madison had learned the lyrics by heart. She chuckled. "Never rescued anyone with chains on their boots."

"Yeah, well, I've never wanted to be rescued so bad that I gave my car keys to a complete stranger." She looked at Madison for a while, then smiled. "You look harmless enough though. Are you?"

Madison turned her green eyes to the woman and held them there. "Absolutely not."

Dani let her head fall back on the headrest and smiled. "Where are you taking me?"

"My place," Madison answered. "Give them some time to calm down a bit then we'll go back for my car. Sound all right?"

"Perfect."

"Just imagine," Mrs. Langford told her husband a few days later. "Taking home a complete stranger. And MTV trash like that too. Roger said he saw her

9

up there when he started mowing the pastures yesterday, just sitting on that deck with her guitar. And not one decent sound coming out of her either."

Every closed society has its secret meeting places. The Summer House was just one more government-kept garrison used by the Intelligence community, by bureaucrats with decisions to make, by separate agencies with separate agendas and a single objective: the planning of a successful operation.

The house was snuggled tightly in a thick patch of Virginia woods, a massive white brick edifice with around the clock security. A helicopter landing pad was buried in a small clearing a few hundred yards away and recently a golf cart had been added to shuttle the aging Director of Central Intelligence to the front door. Air space was restricted in the area, and on more than one occasion bewildered Sunday pilots had found themselves trying to explain to some very skeptical security people why they had wandered off their flight plan.

The library was used for meetings, a long room with polished wood walls, a conference table in the center, and greenhouse windows at the far end with bullet resistant glass so thick that it blurred the view. Mitchell Colby, the Director of Central Intelligence, sat with his back to those windows.

Marge Price sat facing him, letting her mind stray as the others filed in and did their usual hand-shaking. Outside, an armed security guard passed by the window — one of perhaps fifty regulars with bulging jackets and grave faces.

James Jefferies was on hand today, which came as a surprise to the old Director. The Secretary of State was up to his ears with the problems in the Middle East and was rarely available for operational planning sessions here at home.

From the Central Intelligence Agency, Deputy Director Fred Nolan. And Warren Moss, senior analyst for Operations, a man Marge Price studied with interest. She had seen so many self-serving men like Moss pass through this room, hanging on for all they were worth to whatever coattails they could reach. But he was intelligent, white, male, and loaded with political savvy. Warren Moss would go far, and even now Marge watched him carefully choose the seat that the former Deputy Director of Operations had always used.

"Remember, Mitchell," James Jefferies told the DCI once the meeting got underway. "It wasn't a State agent who blew the Peru network sky high. It was one of yours. Now Peru's my problem. Sendero Luminoso is moving closer to Lima, and the Peruvian government's too weak or too scared or too damn corrupt to do anything about it. If they take Lima, there'll be no way to control the flow of drugs."

"We're an Intelligence gathering agency, James," Fred Nolan interjected in his usual moderate tone. "We can't go to war with the traffickers. Our job is collecting and distributing Intelligence."

11

"Yes, well, from where I sit there's been damn little collecting or distributing," Jefferies said. "This is an election year. The President wants results."

Mitchell Colby pursed his lips and folded his big hands in his lap. He was a large man, with thin silver hair and scarlet veins on his nose. "We're talking about an organization that's got control of a third of the countryside, and that includes the coca growing regions. Most of the police and government officials have deserted their posts outside the cities. The Sendero has killed a thousand people this year alone. Seventeen thousand since nineteen-eighty."

"So you're telling me there's nothing we can do?" Jefferies demanded.

The Director shook his head "I'm saying that if you have to work around re-election politics, the President's expectations are unrealistic. You could hurt the Sendero maybe, but you can't invade a sovereign nation and wage war against them. And that's the only way you'll ever get *total* control of the situation."

Jefferies frowned and rubbed the stubble on his chin. "If you've got ideas, let's hear them."

"A few quick strike operations aimed at the processing centers might do it," Colby replied. "Shut down some supply lines, cost them a little money, and scare the hell out of the people processing the stuff. Make it a little harder for the traffickers to get volunteers. At the same time we start a grassroots movement aimed at Lima. Shake things up a little. Get the government into gear and loosen the Sendero hold over the people. Who better to do that than my agency? We've started a few prairie fires, James. Just look at Europe. We lit that match and now the Wall's crumbled."

The Secretary shook his head. "You had your chance in Lima."

"Please, sir, if I may," Warren Moss said mildly, looking at Colby for approval then turning to Jefferies. "The problem is that we've never really had a fair chance at all. What we had was a mole inside this agency selling us out to every service in the world, blowing our people to anyone that would listen, and even with all of that we've managed some amazing operations. Just imagine what we can accomplish now that we've cleaned house."

He took a drink from his water glass and opened the file in front of him. "We've known for months that the Lima network died long ago. The mole tore it down little by little, filled Peru with burned out agents. Now we can rebuild. New faces. Experienced agents with the talent and background for this kind of operation. If we're allocated the funds, I estimate we could have a sizable resistance movement going that could feed itself in three months."

Director Colby leaned back in his chair and gave a nod of approval to his rising star. Fred Nolan watched the Secretary carefully, and Marge Price looked out the window. The Secretary had not taken his eyes off Warren Moss. He asked, "What about you, Nolan? You think you can get in and out without a mess? Set something up that wouldn't require continued U.S. involvement?"

The Deputy Director was a very ordinary looking man, slightly rounded in build, nearly bald with a pleasant face that belied his drive. No one in or out of the agency had ever expected Fred Nolan would go so far. He was a follower, they had said, not cut out to be a leader. But Fred Nolan had carved out a path for himself all the way to the top of the Intelligence section.

He faced the Secretary now over a cup of cold coffee and half a doughnut. "We'd need some kind of support structure in place for some time to come. We can't simply strike the match and walk away. But basic support requires minimal involvement." He thought for a moment. "We did it in Czechoslovakia and we did it in East Germany. I think we can do it in Peru."

Jefferies got up and walked to the window with his hands in his pockets. He stood there for a while then turned back to the group. "Okay, whatever you need, but State picks the head agent for the Lima operation."

Director Colby placed the flat of his hand on the table and growled, "I can't run an effective operation using a State operative. The case officer has to be CIA."

"The case officer we had in mind *is* CIA," Marge assured him.

"McGuire," Jefferies added.

At this Fred Nolan smiled and leaned back in his chair.

Warren Moss cleared his throat and looked at the Secretary. "McGuire's hard to control, Mr. Secretary. Too unpredictable. She's been put on extended leave."

The Secretary of State bent forward, rested both palms on the table and looked at Moss. "Get McGuire, would you Mitchell? And get things moving. Time's wasting."

CHAPTER TWO

Near the city of Huancayo, the heart of Peru's breadbasket, a mere one hundred miles from Lima, workers at the SAIS Cahuide went about their daily routines with no possible idea of the horror the day would bring. Many of the workers had spent their lives here, were very old. Some had not yet reached their teens. But all of them were grateful for the work, grateful for the chance to help feed their families in a country where inflation had reached nearly nine thousand percent. SAIS Cahuide, a thriving private co-op with several hundred employees and a hundred thousand head of livestock, was the largest employer in the region and the producer of nearly fifteen thousand badly needed liters of milk per day.

Jose Muro had been here since he was fifteen years old. He was now twenty-one and married. His wife, Liliana, also worked at the co-op, though her job carried with it a bit more prestige. Liliana Muro was one of over a hundred low-level administrators employed by SAIS Cahuide.

Jose was in one of the huge milking barns when the initial shots were fired. At first, over the equipment noise and voices and mooing cows, it was no more than a sharp pop-pop-pop. Then it happened again, longer this time, louder, unmistakable.

Someone in the barn yelled, *Sendero, Sendero,* and others clambered to a long row of narrow windows that ran the length of the building. A column of guerrillas with ammunition belts crisscrossing their chests and machine guns in their hands marched towards the milking barns.

Near the offices, Jose saw a large group of people huddled together, surrounded by a band of at least fifty guerrillas.

"Liliana," he muttered, and a stabbing panic sliced through him. The guerrillas were firing shots into the air, and with each blast, he could see the terror on the faces of the employees. *Where is she?*

He dashed towards one of the exits, his mind racing, his head throbbing as if he had been hit with a hammer. But before he reached the doors, a group of gunmen crashed through, firing their machine guns in the air. The guns stopped suddenly and one of them shouted, "If you do not cooperate, you will die. Walk outside now and join the others on the hill."

One of the men tried to escape through a side door, but a gunman leveled his machine gun and cut the man in half before he set one foot on the ground outside.

Jose could think of nothing now but Liliana, nothing but cooperating with the terrorists so he could get to Liliana safely.

A group of perhaps one hundred and fifty workers were herded unceremoniously out of the barn. They were half way to the small hill where the others were being held when the killing began.

There was no great passion displayed by the attackers even then, no fanatical slogans shouted by crazed extremists. It was methodical and deliberate, all part of a well-planned attack. It started with the animals — row after row gunned down. And then Jose saw one of the killers walk into the crowd and come out with four people. One he recognized as a technical adviser. The others were administrators. One of them was Liliana.

He started running towards them, yelling her name, pleading with the guerrillas not to shoot. He saw the man point the gun, heard the barrage of bullets, and saw Liliana drop like a battered rag doll.

He was still running, screaming they told him later, though in his memory there were no sounds. There was only Liliana. Liliana falling. Liliana dying.

He remembered the gunman turning to him sharply as he ran closer, remembered with shame that his own knees had buckled in fear at the sight of the gun, remembered crawling on his stomach to Liliana.

The siege lasted several days. The guerrillas herded away the animals they had left for themselves, and enlisted help from the workers in destroying the milking equipment and tractors piece by piece. The barns and offices were burned, and those who did not cooperate fully were starved or shot on the spot.

The day the Sendero disappeared back into the mountains, Jose buried Liliana and started for the small town of Quinches where his friend, Liliana's brother, lived.

Enrique Navarro listened to Jose's story without a word, but Jose saw the tears in his dark eyes, saw the fury sweep over his handsome face as he listened to how his sister had been murdered, how others were starved and shot, how the animals were killed or taken, how the co-op was dismantled so that no one could scratch out a living any longer.

And when Jose had finished, Enrique drew a breath and put his arm around him. "Go with me to Huancayo. The pain is fresh there. The people will listen. It must stop, my brother. Someone must stand up and say *enough*."

The daughter of a Quechua Indian mother and a Spanish father, Paulina Holgodo was born in south-central Los Angeles two months after her parents fled Peru in search of a richer life. America had promised the Holgodos a second chance, a new life. America had received them with open arms and a pledge of freedom. And here they struggled and here they remained poor. Here they buried both their sons, one from a drug overdose, the other slain in gang violence six months later. Here they drove their only daughter to the bus station and solemnly waved goodbye, and then thanked God that Paulina had gotten out alive.

"Go to the army," her father had told her. "It is the only way out."

The army had noticed Paulina in her second year of enlistment. She was tough, efficient, she paid attention. Now, a veteran of six years, Staff Sergeant Paulina Holgodo had successfully completed Ranger School, something few women ever had the chance to do, and had come out of the Airborne School for Paratroopers in Ft. Benning, Georgia with the distinguished silver airborne pin.

In the off hours, while her friends gathered in a dusty little bar called Henry's, Paulina could usually be found in the gym working on her concentration skills with a martial arts instructor, or strength training with free weights. It was in the gym that Lieutenant Wilkes had first noticed her.

Paulina was five-six perhaps, and very determined in her white karate ghi. She had just thrown the platoon sergeant on the mat, and Wilkes saw her smiling victoriously as she stood over him, holding out a hand. She likes winning, Wilkes noted with satisfaction, and scribbled her name on a scrap of paper and stuffed it into his pocket.

Over the next forty-eight hours, the Lieutenant watched her work on the machines in the gym, clocked her when she showed twelve raw recruits how to handle an obstacle course, saw her take a group of baby-faced privates on a staged night raid that was as slick in the planning as any he had ever seen. Her background file, which he had received days before he came here, had already told him that she met other necessary requirements. She was fluent in Spanish and Quechua, was of Peruvian descent, had had two brothers killed in drug-related violence, and displayed extraordinary physical ability. This, combined with what he had seen in the last two days, convinced him to make the call to Langley.

The paperwork managed to get through army bureaucracy at surprising speed. Within a week, Paulina Holgodo and nine others from different divisions whom Lieutenant Wilkes had watched with interest, were dropped off in a nameless swamp where they would endure the rigors of jungle training. None of the group knew why he or she was there, knew why they had been chosen. But they had all noticed certain interesting similarities among them.

On the tenth day, Lieutenant Wilkes sent for Paulina. "At ease, Sergeant," the Lieutenant told her. He was sitting on the edge of a cot in the medical tent. "Sit down. I have a question for you."

"Yes, sir," Paulina answered, taking the adjacent cot.

"What are you doing here?" Wilkes asked, and watched a bewildered expression cross her serious face.

"A training exercise, sir."

But the Lieutenant didn't seem satisfied with her answer. "I'll tell you what you're doing. You're busting your ass for nothing, Holgodo. Army policy doesn't let women do what you're trained to do."

Paulina blinked but never looked away.

"How would you like a chance to do what you're trained to do?"

"I'd like that, sir."

He stood and walked to the door of the tent. "Why did you join the army?" he asked without turning.

"It was a way out of L.A. An education. But you know that already. Don't you, sir?"

Wilkes smiled slightly and turned. He was holding an ink pen, tapping it against the flat of one hand. "I'd like you to be part of a very special group. It'll be a challenge. If you're interested, you'll leave for Panama in two hours. You'll get your orders there. There's no mandatory time in this outfit. You want out when the mission's over, you're out. You can go back to your division, stay with us or go civilian. And, if you're not interested in any of it, you go back today and this conversation never happened."

Paulina nodded. "Understood, sir."

Wilkes went back to the cot and sat down. He placed the palms of his hands on his thighs and leaned forward as if he had a secret. "I gotta tell you, Holgodo, you're good. I watched you last night during the exercise. Out there in the pitch dark, you moved like a cat. You've got good instincts, kid. You almost found me. You knew I was there, didn't you?"

Sergeant Holgodo allowed herself a slight smile. "I didn't know it was you, sir, but I knew we were being observed."

"Are you interested?" the Lieutenant asked.

Paulina had first realized there was something different about this training mission when her orders had been hand-delivered in a sealed envelope by the platoon sergeant, something that had never happened. And then, before dawn, Paulina had been picked up and quietly carried away by military transport. The operation had CIA written all over it.

She stood and faced the Lieutenant, realizing with some amusement that he probably wasn't a Lieutenant at all. "Thank you, sir. I'll pack my gear for Panama."

Wilkes frowned. "I'm not *demanding* a volunteer, Holgodo. This is something you need to think about."

"With respect, sir. I've been thinking about it for ten days," Paulina answered. "We're all Latino. We all speak Spanish. We're training in a jungle. And we all, all ten of us, sir, have lost people close to us because of drugs. It wasn't hard to put together. You're going after the traffickers."

"I certainly can't confirm that, Sergeant," Lieutenant Wilkes snapped. "Has anyone in authority confirmed that idea to you?"

"No, sir. I just wanted you to know that if that's what's happening, we're ready."

She heard the car before it was close enough to see, despite Dani's music from the house and the distant growl of a tractor in one of the fields. Even now, safely in exile, there was a part of her that never stopped listening.

She stood on the shaded side of the deck putting the finishing touches on a new kitchen window. She listened another moment then walked around the front. A cloud of dust rose up over the hill and she saw the blue sedan rounding the bend towards the house.

Marge Price was not a pretty woman in the conventional sense. She was a bit too heavy, her face a bit too wide and severe and lined by every emotional wound she had ever suffered. But when she stepped out of the car, she was quite a lovely sight in Madison's eyes.

She climbed the steps with that quiet, weightless walk only stocky women seem to manage so perfectly, and hugged Madison, then pulled back to inspect her at arm's length.

Madison was barefoot, in khaki shorts and a shirt with the sleeves rolled to the elbow. She was tan and muscled. Marge smiled and glanced at the house when she heard Dani's guitar. "I hear you have a guest."

Madison laughed. "Ah, so you've met Mrs. Langford, Queen of Helen proper and rumormonger extraordinaire. Gave you directions and told you her tales, did she?" She looked back at the house and shrugged. "Dani needed quiet to work on her music, and I'd had too much of it. Rescued each other in a way, I think. Nothing serious, really. Great sex and a bit of fun. Thinks I'm a bloody journalist, by the way. Like to meet her?"

"I'd like to talk first," Marge said, seriously.

Every field agent in the world has his or her own technique for concealing emotion. Madison's was in her utter stillness. Marge had seen it before. A sort of over-wakefulness that made her body so tranquil when her mind was engaged.

"The Company sent you?" she asked at last and very quietly, while those bright, unflinching eyes set themselves on Marge.

"That and I wanted to know how you are."

Madison put an arm on her shoulder and led her to a table and chairs on the deck. She picked up a pack of cigarettes from the table and jarred one loose. "So, let's have it, shall we? They've sent you with a message? Do they love me this week? Or am I to be flogged?" Small talk had never been easy for Madison.

Marge chuckled and sat down. "It's an assignment. I'm supposed to give you a briefcase. It's in the car."

Madison half smiled and walked to the railing. "Thought I'd been banished for good," she muttered, remembering her return to Langley six months ago. She had headed for Director Colby's office only to be stopped by his assistant and told Colby was unavailable — but he wanted her to know there was always a place for her at the Farm, the CIA's training center at Camp Peary — called Kindergarten in the Company jargon.

She remembered the silence that hung over the long corridors like an iron curtain as news of her return spread, remembered the averted eyes as she stepped into the Company dining room — the woman who had brought down their beloved Prince. For it was Madison McGuire who only weeks before had exposed one of the Central Intelligence Agency's top guns as a double agent, Madison McGuire who had pursued the traitor relentlessly and helped strike the final blow. And it was Madison who, for all her toil, was given only an icy nod of approval and a leave of absence while the Company endured the chaos of reorganization and tried to forget her victory. Their trust had been shattered, Madison knew, and she was a visible reminder. For in our society whistle blowers are rarely rewarded and even less so in the secret world.

"Why didn't you stay at the Farm?" Marge asked. "Walking away like that didn't earn you any friends."

Washington, D.C. and the surrounding area had been many things for Madison — a landing strip, a paycheck, an office, and, sometimes, briefly, even a lover. But it could never be home. She turned from the railing and looked at Marge. "Don't have the patience for it anymore. Trying to convince a bunch of kindergartners there's still something to spy on. Peace is breaking out everywhere, you know. Poor babies are terribly worried."

Marge laughed. Madison's British accent coupled with the fact that she forgot her pronouns part of the time had always amused her greatly. "Any luck convincing them?" The world was changing. Cold Warriors were emerging from the thaw, shaking off the chill of the past, unsure of what would come next.

New alliances or new threats? Madison had asked this of her tidy little group one day, then scanned their earnest faces while they contemplated the New World. There had not been a blink or a cough in the room that day.

Madison sat sideways on the railing now, arms

folded, looking at Marge. "Haven't done what I've done just to be put out to pasture at the Farm."

"You know," Marge said thoughtfully, "someone once said that the truth might become more popular if it weren't always stating such ugly facts. You knew there was a mole in the agency, and you pestered them until they gave you a free hand to do something about it. Which was the right thing to do. But you're a woman and you knew it first. *That* was your sin. They look at you and all their short-comings look right back at them. You expected gratitude?"

"How did you know?" Madison asked dryly.

"I know you, Madison. One day you'll stop trying to live up to your father."

It was true. Marge knew Madison in ways no one else could. For Marge Price was the one person who had access to all areas of Madison's life — the professional and the deeply personal. It had been Marge who had counseled her when her secret life had once betrayed her. Marge, a surrogate mother with a top secret security clearance. Marge, a specialist in the psychology of field operatives for the State Department's Intelligence section, who had guided her gently back into the world. And it was Marge who understood how the stories of her father's heroics had shadowed her own career, how the inevitable comparisons had haunted her, compelled her to take risks, to be as good, then better. Fable or myth, the legend of Jake McGuire was a significant part of the Agency's unwritten history and quite something for Madison to live with.

Marge reached for one of Madison's cigarettes and then watched as Madison walked into the house.

She saw her pause at the couch where Dani sat with a pencil stuck behind one ear and a guitar on her lap, she saw Madison stoop to kiss her forehead lightly then disappear into the kitchen. When she came back with drinks, Marge crossed her legs and asked as casually as she could manage, "Have you called Terry?"

Madison shook her head. "How is she?"

"Worried about you. It's been months. It wouldn't hurt to call." Marge waited in vain for the flash of temper, the surge of protest she expected, but instead Madison collected her drink and retreated quietly to the deck railing. She gazed down as if she were contemplating the fall. Looking at her in profile, Marge thought she seemed especially remote.

She stepped alongside her and massaged her shoulders. "I know you left Terry to protect her. Because your world was dangerous for her. It was an admirable decision, but not one that will be easy to live with."

Madison turned sharply. "An admirable decision," she repeated with a slight laugh. "I believed that at first too. Convinced myself I'd committed an utterly selfless act. And, oh, how easily I slip into the martyr role. Did you know that about me too? Truth is, I left Terry because I can't give up my work. Most selfish thing I've ever done in my life."

Marge sighed. "Torturing yourself won't help."

Madison jiggled her drink and watched the ice swirl around the glass. "I have a photo of her," she began quietly. "It's summer and she's on the beach barefoot, clutching something she's found in the sand. I don't even remember what it was now. She's in white shorts, looking directly into the camera and there's something in her eyes. Something in the way she looked at me that day." Madison lifted her head slowly to Marge. "She knew. She knew I'd hurt her even then." She paused and took an enormous breath. "Oh how the perils of spying pale to the dangers of love, huh?" She smiled and wrapped her arm around Marge's waist. "Come. It's time you met Dani."

CHAPTER THREE

The Washington Post: *As the war against drugs continues, President Brown, in an effort to fulfill a campaign promise, announced today a new plan called The Andean Initiative. State Department bulldozers will begin tomorrow cutting landing strips along the Upper Huallaga River, three hundred miles northeast of Lima, where over half the world's coca, the raw ingredient for cocaine, is produced. From there the Peruvian Army could launch paramilitary operations against the valley's coca-processing centers and the illegal airstrips used by traffickers to fly coca paste to Colombia. The president denied that American military presence would be required, but said, "We have to nip the problem in the bud." An unidentified Pentagon source said that any military operations, if mandated by changing circumstances, would be "in addition to and separate from current joint DEA-Peruvian National Police operations and would be in the planning stage for quite some time."*

"So then she pushes her way through the crowd and whispers for me to follow her if I want out." Dani Stone laughed and cocked her head towards Madison, who stood at the kitchen sink. "I mean just look at that woman. Who wouldn't follow her? Right? And the whole time I just kept thinking, you know, there must be a song in this somewhere."

Chuckling, Marge Price pushed her dinner plate aside. "Sounds like you both needed a diversion."

"Yeah." Dani nodded thoughtfully and ran one finger around the rim of her wine glass. "I have to leave in a couple days though and Madison's got that assignment. You must be with the newspaper too." Marge stared at her blankly for a moment, and Dani said, "I mean, I just assumed you're with the paper since you told her about the assignment and all."

Madison came out from the kitchen, smiling. "You know, Marge, I hear the memory's the first thing to go. No more wine for you."

* * * * *

It was much later when Madison crept into the living room with the locked briefcase and switched the lights on dim. Marge had left an hour ago, and Dani had said goodnight even earlier. Like most people who had too little time to themselves, Dani Stone was very protective of her privacy.

"I don't know how much they told you in that briefcase," Marge had told Madison when they walked to her car, "but the assignment is Peru and the Lima Station Chief was killed three weeks ago. Be careful, Madison."

Madison set the briefcase on the coffee table and dialed in the combination. Inside, she found a folder labeled: OPERATION MAXIM 1 — CLASSIFIED EYES ONLY. The folder contained two escape passports. She found flight instructions and an airline ticket from Atlanta's Hartsfield airport to Tampa. There she would be picked up for briefing.

She closed the case, sat back on the couch and shut her eyes. A calm washed gently over her, the same self-imposed stillness Marge had seen, a kind of clarity of mind that always came before an assignment. *This is what I was trained for. This is what I was born to do.*

She heard a sound and opened her eyes. Dani stood at the doorway in a T-shirt that came to her knees, her hands behind her back. "Come," Madison said, but she didn't move.

"Tell me if I'm wrong or if it's none of my business," Dani said. "But I really got some weird vibes when Marge was here. I mean, I liked her and everything and she was nice, but I had the feeling she was sizing me up the whole time. You know what I mean? Comparing me to someone else. There was someone else, wasn't there?"

"Yes," Madison said quietly, looking away.

"And you still love her?"

"God, it seems like a lifetime ago now. Another existence. It's over."

Dani looked at Madison for a moment. "Where are you going when you leave here? Your assignment, I mean. What part of the world?"

"Siberia," Madison answered with a smile.

Dani flipped the light switch, and Madison saw her in silhouette approaching the couch, saw her slip the T-shirt over her head in the half light, saw that she was naked underneath. She guided Madison back on the couch and began her ascent, locking her knees around Madison's sides, first unbuttoning Madison's shirt, then her shorts.

"You know," she whispered in slow, grainy tones, and her deep voice sent a chill over Madison, "here in the dark I could be anyone. Someone you've wanted. Someone you've fantasized about. Or maybe just a stranger you've never seen before. Someone you'll never see again. A stranger in the night that you can't see now." She leaned very close to Madison's ear. "A stranger in the night that you can't touch." She lifted Madison's hands to her breasts and Madison felt the steel clamp around her wrists like desire, heard the locks tumble into place.

Surrender had never been simple for Madison. The implications were too great — giving over to another power, a submission that was against her nature entirely — but tonight she closed her eyes and indulgently relinquished control. She let Dani take her, let Dani secure her wrists, let Dani draw her closer.

She felt Dani kissing her, felt the length of Dani's lean body pressing against her, felt Dani's hands under her clothes. Dani whispering. Now kneeling, guiding Madison's mouth closer. Now crying out. Now biting Madison's nipples. Now plunging a hand into Madison's shorts.

She was everywhere at once, and for the first time in her life, Madison McGuire yielded without restraint.

His name was Harry Carson, but he had used many names in his twenty years with the Central Intelligence Agency. A few days ago he had been Lieutenant John Wilkes of the United States Army.

Today Carson was conducting his first visual evaluation of the major coca growing regions of Peru. He had seen all the maps, studied them, been over with the insertion team the charts and schedules, check points and emergency codes, but it had been a long time since Harry Carson had seen this kind of jungle.

Soon after leaving the town of Oracuza in the small aircraft, he watched the eastern slopes of the Andes sink sharply into the Amazon River basin, dipping and falling unevenly into a dense tropical forest, into miles of trackless jungle.

"That's it," the pilot told him in Spanish when they had reached the Upper Huallaga Valley. The pilot, Gilberto Salaverria, was Peruvian, his business was flying and most of his customers were in the drug business. He had been a casual CIA asset for three years. "And there's the Huallaga River. Not many landmarks down there unless you count the rubber trees." Salaverria laughed and Carson turned away, looking out his window.

Operation MAXIM-2, Carson thought, gets underway in three days. In seventy-two hours those kids will be plowing through that jungle with sixty pounds of gear on their backs. *Jesus, what fucking egghead analyst convinced the Director that this was gonna work?*

"How about the processing sites?" he asked, looking back at the pilot.

"Deeper in the jungle mostly, but they move all the time. Here one day, gone the next. But the airstrips. We can see a few of those. Not too close though. They do not like it if I get too close. Perhaps if I understood more about what you are looking for, I could be of more help."

"You're doing fine," Carson answered. He didn't trust the man, could not trust any man who made his living off the drug lords. The pilot played both sides, Carson suspected, and he wasn't going to give him any ammunition to sell to the other side.

"Some advice, Señor Carson," the pilot said suddenly. "If your bosses are planning to send people down there, it is best to remember that you must understand the jungle to survive the jungle."

But Carson knew that already, and the thought of another war in the jungle sent a sudden, wrenching pain through his stomach. He had spent two years in Viet Nam, and he had learned as the world had learned that you cannot do for a country what it does not want to do for itself.

He thought of the young soldiers he had recruited, remembered their faces as they boarded the C-130 Hercules for the U.S. Southern Command in Panama. They were eager and determined, and no one — not Carson, not the CIA analysts with all their charts and maps, not even the Director himself — had had any real idea of what they were walking into.

On the outskirts of Huancayo, Enrique Navarro walked the grounds of what had once been the SAIS Cahuide, surveying the scene with disgust — the gutted smoke-stained buildings, the stench of rotting animal carcasses, the flies, the hopelessness.

Word of the attack had spread through the mountains, and peasants with horse-drawn wagons had left their farms to join the workers in an attempt to clean up the mess. An old man leaned against one of the dismantled tractors, sobbing into his hands. "They will come back," he kept saying. "They will come back and kill us all."

Enrique climbed to the top of the tractor and tried to get the workers' attention. Finally, he withdrew the pistol tucked into the back of his pants and fired one shot into the air. There was a brief panic. Shots had been fired here not long ago and the terror was still fresh in their minds. "Do you want to cower here in fear for the rest of your lives, waiting for the Sendero to come back?" Enrique

Navarro shouted, and all eyes turned to him. Slowly, mostly out of curiosity, they began to gather round him.

A woman in the crowd called out, "Who are you? A stranger who comes here after the damage is done to call us cowards? What have you lost?" There was a hiss of whispers. Heads nodded in agreement.

"I am Enrique Navarro. A farmer from Quinches, and I have lost my sister," he said, and a hush washed over the crowd. "I have lost what you have lost. I've lost my country." He paused and his gaze swept over them. "And where is the Sendero now?" he demanded. "They were the people's movement. Remember? They would protect us, make work for us, help us feed our families. Only promises, all of it. But we believed them. We helped them. We are a trusting people. Now that they have taken everything away from us, where are they? They're rich from the drug money. They are fat from the cattle they've stolen from you."

"No," a man shouted, pushing his way through the crowd. "They have not taken from us. They have taken from the pigs who support our corrupt government. It is part of the plan. Society must be destroyed before it can be rebuilt. We suffer now, but when the Sendero takes the government, then we will all prosper. This is the path to change."

"I understand the need for change," Enrique answered. "I have no argument with the Sendero there. They have been right about many things. Our people *have* been exploited for centuries. Our government *is* corrupt. There must be a fundamental change in our country. But what happens if they take power? Have they clearly defined their

36

programs for us? No, they have not. Have they even begun a plan to meet the people's needs? No, they have not. Are they anything more to us than an idealistic promise? Are they anything more to us now than fear?"

"And what do you promise us?" A boy of no more than sixteen called out. "What can you offer us when they hold all the money and all the power?"

"Look back," Enrique shouted. "History has shown us that people will only endure oppression for so long. People will only live in fear for so long. It doesn't matter who has the money and the power. The Peruvian spirit will triumph." He smiled. "My mother used to say that Peru has two spirits. The Indian and the Spanish. The condor and the bull. But in this war, we're one, and together we are many."

"And what will we fight this war with?" someone yelled. "Our spirits?" A wave of laughter swept over the group. Enrique jumped off the tractor and headed into the crowd.

"Yes," he answered, working his way to the center. "With our spirits. With our hands and our words. With sticks and rocks and guns if we must. Because if we want to save ourselves, we must fight for Peru. Not the President's Peru. Not the Sendero's Peru. Not the Peru of the Colombian drug lords. Our Peru."

The man who had shouted the praises of the Shining Path stepped forward. He was forty-five perhaps, with dark leathery skin, and an unlit cigarette between his teeth. "You expect these people to fight the Sendero? Peasants and farmers?"

"I ask them only to fight for what is theirs,"

Enrique answered. "No matter who tries to take it away."

The man laughed and shook his head. "They will be crushed. You will be crushed."

Enrique looked at the faces around him. "So now the same people who promised to save us so many years ago threaten to crush us. Is this what they've made of their power? Are we the part of society they want destroyed? They kill our animals. They burn our farms. They starve us into the cities. Is this how they plan to save Peru? Is this what you wanted?"

The answer from the crowd was a resounding "NO!"

Enrique turned back to the man. "Tell your Sendero friends that we will fight for what is ours."

The enormous, walled home sat on a smooth grassy hilltop overlooking the valley that was the city of Medellin. All the trees and shrubbery had been cleared, leaving a clean line of sight to the valley so that no one could approach without being seen.

Just outside the massive stone wall that circled the house, two armed guards patrolled a dirt path. Another sat on a stool at the gate, and inside the wall two more made regular patrols around the house. One guard was positioned as lookout on the roof at the helicopter landing pad to insure a safe escape for his employer if it ever became necessary. So far it had never been necessary. The owner of the house was one of the richest and most powerful men in the Cartel. He had never been arrested, had never even come close.

Inside, Julio Bermudez sat with his feet propped on his desk and chuckled as he read the reprinted article from the *Washington Post*. There had been so many printed threats from the United States over the years that he had ceased to be frightened by any of them.

Bermudez was fifty and fit. He was not a drinker, only smoked marijuana occasionally, had given up cigarettes twenty years ago, and never, ever used the cocaine he exported to Europe and the United States. He had made his fortune twenty-five years ago and had kept it. He watched it grow as the demand for drugs grew, and he knew, as the United States knew, that anything short of a full-scale invasion could do him no lasting harm. The Colombian police were no match for his power. Many civilians, politicians, and a good number of the military enjoyed a safe, comfortable lifestyle because of their affiliation with Bermudez, and no one was prepared to risk his displeasure. For Julio Bermudez took even the slightest betrayal very seriously indeed — the punishment was always death, on occasion even delivered by Bermudez himself. The prospect of death at his hand seemed to be an excellent deterrent.

"The Andean Initiative," he muttered as he scanned the newspaper. "Such an ambitious man, this President Brown." He looked up at his security chief who sat across the room with a section of newspaper in his hands. "Get in touch with

Carlotta," Bermudez ordered. "Tell her to find out about this Andean Initiative. President Brown is getting too arrogant, I think. Time to remind him who he's dealing with."

CHAPTER FOUR

Madison's plane landed in Tampa at dusk. She was waiting in baggage claim for her one suitcase to pop out of the chute when a middle-aged man with a plain face approached. She had seen him when she entered the area, standing with a claim ticket in his hand, watching the bags circle the island and occasionally glancing at his ticket as if he might not recognize his bag without it.

Watchers come in all shapes and sizes, Madison reflected when she spotted him. But there is one thing they all seem to have in common — an air about them that says there is nothing else in the world they would rather be doing, a tolerance of inertia that can only be learned. It is this that betrays them to the trained spotter.

"It's supposed to rain tonight," he said, casually. "I'm Jack. Are you vacationing?"

Madison glanced at him. He was a full head taller than she, with light hair and eyes. "Yes. I'm here for seven days."

He nodded. "Hope you brought a raincoat."

"An umbrella," Madison answered, and then in order to complete the prearranged code sequence, she added, "A raincoat too."

He smiled and lowered his voice. "Jesus, I wonder who thought that one up. Come on. We have a puddle-jumper waiting for us. Damn thing'll put your heart in your throat. Hope it wasn't a dinner flight you took."

They had flown northwest for a very brief time when the pilot put down on a poorly lit dirt strip. Jack didn't get out when they landed. He simply nodded and slammed the door after her.

She walked to the edge of the landing strip and watched the plane get turned around. It took several hundred feet before it got up enough power to sputter off the ground, and then it barely cleared the trees. Madison wondered if Jack was cursing the pilot as he had when they landed.

The runway lights went out immediately after the takeoff, presumably by remote control, and Madison waited in the dark for several minutes before she saw headlights approaching. When the driver parked the Jeep, he did not dim the lights. Madison had to squint to make out the figure walking towards her.

Greg Allen Abbott, head of the State Department's Intelligence section, was thin as a wire, his face clean-shaven and narrow, his eyes bright, intelligent. He was also one of the best controllers Madison had ever worked with — alert, conscientious, focused.

He extended a manicured hand. "Good to see you, Madison. How long's it been?"

Madison took his hand and held it. "A couple of years, I think. Thought you'd gone on to bigger things by now. Still cloak and dagger, are you, Abbott?"

He laughed and took Madison's bag. "Same old thing. Pounding away at State. You hungry?"

Madison shook her head. "Dinner flight."

Where the government's clandestine agencies lacked creativity in other areas, they excelled at finding a multitude of secret places to prep agents and pavement artists, listeners and killers and couriers. Madison had been instructed in silent killing on an anonymous east coast island with white beaches. She had studied secret writing and invisible inks on a run-down houseboat off the coast of Veracruz, and once she had spent three days in a lighthouse with a Signal Intelligence officer from the NSA. But the barn came as quite a surprise.

Inside, it resembled nothing of a barn. It was modern and well-lit and clean, with partitions dividing it into several separate sections — a large computer room with a line of video screens and communication equipment, two bedrooms with bunk beds, a fully equipped kitchen, a ping-pong table, showers done army style with no dividers and drains built into the floor. Another room held white counters that were cluttered with pliers and tweezers, bits of wire and electrical parts. At the far end, a man in a lab coat named John nodded distractedly when he was introduced to Madison and scribbled something only a pharmacist could read on a chalk board.

A stocky man with ginger hair and eyebrows so blond they were almost nonexistent had greeted them cheerfully at the door. His name was Bob, Abbott said, without bothering about any other explanation as to his presence there except to say that so far Bob had won every match at the ping-pong table. Madison wondered vaguely how many Bobs and Johns she had met in her career, wondered if these men had been hauled in from Langley just for the mission prep or if this was an actual research center that employed them full time — questions that would never be answered. John, she thought, had the look of a Langley researcher from Science and Technology with his white lab coat and his busy hands. But Bob, Bob could be anyone.

A wiry woman with an unhappy scowl motioned for them to step into the computer room. A line of syringes lay on the table beside her. "This the one?" she asked Abbott, then turned unceremoniously to Madison. "I need your left arm and both your hips."

Madison McGuire had faced danger in her life that most people never experienced, but the mere mention of a shot triggered a child's dread in her. She looked at the needles and had to fight the urge to bolt and run.

Abbott smiled, but said nothing to put her at ease. "This is Mary. She's here to give you your gamma globulin immunizations. Typhoid inoculations too. Right, Mary?" He paused and his smile widened. "Typhoid and Mary. How about that? Never thought of it that way before. Anyway, I had mine earlier, and I can tell you one thing. You won't be doing any horseback riding for a while." He laughed and Madison cursed him under her breath as he left the room.

Carlotta Cafferata's training had begun when she was but eighteen years old. In a North African training camp financed by the cartel and used frequently by Shining Path operatives, Carlotta learned the fundamentals of being an Intelligence operative under the former head of Israeli Intelligence. At twenty-one she managed to gain citizenship in the United States after her employer, Julio Bermudez, had made the necessary arrangements. Initially Bermudez's business associates had seen his investment in Carlotta as a gamble. They had not been supportive, insisting that sending Carlotta to the U.S. with no one to watch over her was too much of a risk. How easy it would be for her to fall in love with her life in America, to grow tired of her job, to fall out of love with Bermudez and try to damage his business by sending false Intelligence. All were risks Bermudez had carefully considered. For he was, above all, a careful man.

But Carlotta could do him no real damage. He had always made sure that she knew nothing of the structure of the cartel. She would not even be able to pinpoint the operative training camps on a map. She could give the U.S. nothing but his name. In truth, the authorities knew more about him already than Carlotta would ever know. She could cost him nothing but the few dollars he had invested in her training and support. So he had had nothing to lose and everything to gain. And now Carlotta Caferatta had blossomed into the most productive asset the cartel had ever placed in America.

She had met Les Newman eight months ago in a bar near Capitol Hill where she worked as a bartender. In fact she had met many men there, most of them government officials. Carlotta was the kind of woman that attracted men easily — tall with a small waist and round hips, long dark hair and a child's wide eyes. She spoke perfect English with only a hint of accent, something that had taken her nearly a year to perfect.

She had recognized Les Newman as the assistant Secretary of State immediately. She had let him buy her a drink after work, even let his driver drop her at home, but she had refused his sexual advances for almost a month.

Now he lay in her bed waiting while she mixed their drinks. Outside the kitchen door of her apartment she heard a rustle and knew it was his bodyguard waiting on the back steps to drive him home. She walked softly into the living room and removed a small packet of white powder from her bag and dropped some of it into Newman's drink. *Use just a quarter of it,* Bermudez's security chief had told her. *Not enough to fuck him up real bad. Just enough to loosen his tongue and make him sleepy.*

Carlotta then poured a cup of coffee and cracked the kitchen door. "Hi," she said to the bodyguard who had spent many evenings outside her door. "May be a late night. Thought you could use some coffee."

"Thanks, Carla," the man said with a smile, and took the coffee appreciatively.

She found her lover lying under the top sheet, smiling at her as she walked in. Newman was not a tall man, five-nine perhaps with a broad, hairy chest and light blue eyes. He tried to stay fit, mostly for her, she knew. He felt insecure about his body and often apologized for the middle-aged bulge at his waist. But his work generally sabotaged his plans to exercise and most of his time was spent behind a desk.

"Ah, that's my girl," he said, propping himself on a pillow and patting the space next to him on the bed. "Best drink in town right here." She watched him take the first sip then leaned over to kiss him. They would make love once more, then watch *Nightline* together before he went home to his wife.

Newman liked it that she was interested in the news, and he enjoyed giving her an insider's view of the world. His wife never questioned him about his work, had hardly shown any interest in his career at all. But Carlotta wanted to know everything. No detail was unimportant to her. She had even asked about his office, what it looked like, what it felt like to be so important, and she had squeezed his hand excitedly when he promised to take her there sometime.

"Carla, honey," he said softly. "Why do you insist on living here? In this neighborhood. I worry about you coming home at night. I could get you a nice place out of town and —"

She stroked his thigh gently. "Drink your drink and make love to me. We'll talk later."

Newman smiled. He was falling in love with her, he knew, and he couldn't stop himself.

Typhoid Mary left in the morning and no one, certainly not Madison, was sorry to see her go. She had had the misfortune of sharing a bedroom with the woman, and had listened all night to her breathing from the bunk below. It was more of a gurgling sound really, Madison told Abbott, a nasty sort of asthmatic wheeze. At breakfast Madison suggested Mary give herself a shot in the rear to clear up the snoring, but the humor escaped her and only served to harden the scowl on her face.

Bob, it turned out, was an authority on Peru, and John, as Madison had rightly guessed, was what they called a tinkerer in the Company jargon, a researcher from S&T who helped develop the gadgets of the trade — tiny cameras, microphones, concealable weapons — that cut risks and give the edge to an agent in the field.

For the next seventy-two hours Greg Allen Abbott seemed to make Madison his life's work, spending nearly every waking moment with her, drilling her during their long walks together on contact procedures, listening to her recite number codes for telephone messages while he frustrated himself at the ping-pong table with Bob who was still reigning champion. At lunch they worked on open-code phrases she would use on the street, and in the afternoon reviewed escape procedures they hoped would never be used. Abbott was, as always, attentive and thorough. He liked his agents briefed fully before they set one foot on foreign soil and he did his best to create an environment that would contribute to the learning process. He wanted Madison relaxed and comfortable, didn't want her distracted by schedule changes during the mission preparation, so he encouraged her to stick with her daily routines, meals and exercise at normal times. Madison thought Abbott must shine his brightest when he was working, though she had never really known him apart from his work.

After dinner they joined Bob in the computer room, where he pulled up photographs and files on agents the Company had already placed in the major cities of Peru. He concentrated on Lima in particular, showed her street maps and explained the city. He spoke knowledgeably of the struggle facing Peruvian people, of the economy, the government, the Sendero Luminoso.

"The Shining Path isn't fulfilling the people's needs and the government isn't doing it," he said. "The place is ripe for these little resistance movements that keep springing up. The problem is keeping them going. Look at this." He typed something into his computer and pointed to the wide screen mounted on the wall. A grainy still-photograph of a man appeared. "Jose Echevera," he explained. "Started a resistance movement two years ago. Killed by government troops during a riot outside the Presidential Palace in Lima. The movement died with him." Again he typed. "And this was Cruz Luscombe, leader of the Peruvian Liberation Front. Killed trying to protect farmers at Cerro de Pasco from Shining Path guerrillas. So, you see any new movement is the natural enemy of both the government and the Shining Path." He keyed in another command and looked at Madison. "Just got this in. His name is Enrique Navarro. He's a farmer. Or at least he was. From what we can put together, his sister was killed in the Sendero attack on the co-op outside Huancayo. He left his farm and went up there during the cleanup. Recruited about a hundred people on the spot. He's working the city now, using the same rhetoric. It's working. He's got at least a couple hundred training at one of the farms. Reports say they're poorly armed, in bad physical condition and disorganized as hell, but they plan to try and hold back the guerrillas if they come back to Huancayo. And believe me, they will come back!"

He thought for a moment, plucking at one blond eyebrow with his thumb and index finger. "This movement might be something for us to look at. I mean this guy has put together a couple hundred people in a few days, men and women and kids with sticks and shovels, and he's convinced them that they can take over the government or something. We're talking charisma out the wazoo here."

"Where's his file?" Madison asked. "What's his background?"

"A big question mark so far," Greg Abbott answered. "We're getting all that's available right now. You'll be the first to know."

"Maybe he's got some background in soldiering," Bob added. "But from the looks of things he's more guts and talk than anything else. And right now he needs help or he'll die out there just like the others."

"Why are you so sure the Sendero will come back to Huancayo?" Madison asked, reaching for a cigarette. Abbott, who hated the smell of her brown cigarettes, moved sulkily to the other side of the room.

"Huancayo is critical for the Shining Path," Bob answered. "It's only a little over a hundred miles from Lima. Once they take Huancayo they plan to circle Lima, cut it off from the rest of the country, take the government. And in time, they'll do it unless they meet some resistance."

"And the people, " Madison said quietly. "What do they want?"

The building was still except for the quiet whir of the air conditioning system and a faint tapping of John in his lab, studiously breaking something down or piecing it together.

Bob punched a few buttons and Navarro's picture disappeared from the screen. He leaned back in his swivel chair and looked at the ceiling for a few moments. "What the people want," he said, spinning around in his chair to Madison, "has never been a primary concern in geopolitics."

* * * * *

In Mitchell Colby's view, White House Chief of Staff Robert Little was a complete ass, a purely political animal who would jump through hoops for whoever held power. In fact, Colby had just shared that opinion with Secretary of State James Jefferies while they waited in Little's White House office for him to arrive. Colby also deeply resented the fact that Robert Little had managed to cut off the direct access to the President he had always enjoyed.

"I mean, Jesus Christ," Colby told Jefferies. "The Chief of Staff shouldn't be privy to this kind of information. We should be briefing the President."

Jefferies smiled. "He's just a buffer. If it all falls to shit tomorrow, the President wants someone between him and covert operations. You notice we didn't see the President's signature on the go-ahead papers. Little is his deniability."

Robert Little's office door opened and the small, tubby man stepped through, smiling the politician's smile he had perfected during his time as governor of Virginia. "Good to see you, James. You too, Mitch." The Chief of Staff was the only person who called the DCI Mitch, and Colby added it to his list of resentments. "Sorry to keep you waiting," Little went on. "The President's in foul humor this morning. We're down another three points in the polls."

The side door of the office opened and a clean-cut steward stepped through with a tray of coffee and bagels. The Chief of Staff dipped his knife into a tub of cream cheese and carefully spread it over his bagel. "Help yourself, gentlemen," Little said. Colby and Jefferies reached for coffee. They had had their breakfast hours ago in a pre-dawn meeting at State. "So, are we ready on Maxim One and Two?"

"Maxim Two," Colby reported reluctantly, "will be underway in less than six hours. They've left Panama for Oracuza. We can stage the drop from there after dark by helicopter."

"Expect any problems going in?" Little asked.

Colby shook his head. "Not since the article in the *Post*. Right now the State Department bulldozers are drawing the attention. If the traffickers expect anything, they think it's going to be initiated from the landing strips State's laying down. We'll slip in at night right into the heart of the jungle. They'll never know we're there."

"Let's just be sure they can never *prove* we were there," Little said, one eye blinking independently of the other in a nervous habit they had all come to expect from the Chief of Staff. "The last thing the President needs right now is rumors of American troops stomping through the jungle." He took a sip from his coffee cup. "You sure these kids won't have a change of heart once they see some action?"

"These people are trained quick-strike operators," Colby answered. "They all have a personal interest in this operation. They're good soldiers and we don't anticipate any security problems."

"And Maxim One?" Robert Little asked, looking to James Jefferies.

"We're finishing up the preparation now," the secretary answered. "State's set up command communications for both ops in Lima and Mitchell's agents are already providing some good intell. They've found somewhere for us to put our money."

He handed over a folder detailing what background had been dug up on the fledgling resistance movement led by Enrique Navarro.

Robert Little thumbed through the file, his small blue eyes traveling quickly over the documents. "This is good. Very good. A small movement capable of making enough noise to distract the Shining Path while we hit them in the jungle."

James Jefferies looked at Mitchell Colby then back at the Chief of Staff. "That's not the objective as I understand it, Robert. The President made it very clear to me when we spoke about this that he wanted to start something long term that would do more than treat the symptoms."

"The objective has changed," Little said, and withdrew a nail file from his desk drawer. "The President understands now that such an ambitious plan may not be possible in an election year. Right now all we want to do is slow the flow of drugs into this country for a while."

"It's a little late to change directions," Jefferies said angrily. "We've done all the leg work on Maxim One. We're ready to go. The rest of the team should be in Peru within hours. Our head agent has instructions to make finding Navarro a priority. Now what the hell are we supposed to do?"

"Nothing's changed in the short term, James," Little answered. "Making contact with the resistance is still a priority. The only real change is that we limit our support in the long term."

"What does that mean?" Jefferies demanded.

"It means," Colby answered dryly, "we give them some toys, help them make some noise, and leave them with their dicks in their hands."

Robert Little's eye had started its blinking again. It was time for new blood in the CIA, he thought. Something he had been telling the President for nearly three years. "I look at it this way. We're giving them a chance. What they do with it when we leave is up to them."

"They won't last a month after we leave unless we do this right," Jefferies said. "Invest some time in training them. Help them set up their operations, their command structure. We have a chance to do something here, Robert. Give us three months and we can make some changes that might very well benefit the United States in the long run."

"You're losing sight of the objective here, James," Robert Little warned. "There won't be a long run for any of us if we don't concentrate on getting the President re-elected."

CHAPTER FIVE

It was dusk and several degrees cooler beyond the wall, but inside the fortress there was no breeze. Six ceiling fans hung low on the lavish terrace of the hacienda and whirled at top speed. A pitcher of water sat in the center of the table and Julio Bermudez watched absently as it shed drops of sweat onto the glass table. His security chief had just delivered the Intelligence he had requested, courtesy of the resourceful Carlotta, and Julio quietly considered his options.

Details on the Andean Initiative were sparse. It seemed that the operation was compartmentalized to such an extent that no one person had all the details at CIA or State Department levels.

Bermudez knew now that State Department bulldozers were clearing jungle landing strips they never intended to use, knew it was a diversionary tactic. He knew that a group of professional soldiers would be dropped into the jungle, exact time and location currently unknown. He had discovered that both the CIA and State Department were involved in an ambitious propaganda operation to discredit the Shining Path and begin a revolt that would slow their progress, discovered the principal agent would be flying into Lima under a British passport, flight origin unknown, name unknown. There were many unknowns. Too many for a cautious man to be comfortable with.

Nicaragua, he thought, El Salvador, Panama were all lessons in the recent history of American aggression. Bermudez knew what happened when American Intelligence began this kind of secretive campaign. Soon they would pour money into opposition groups. Weapons would arrive. More troops. The Shining Path would find themselves in a war around the cities, and that would leave the coca growing regions, where seventy percent of the cartel's profits originated, unprotected while the U.S. dropped more soldiers into the jungle.

"Call my business associates," he told his chief of security. "An emergency council meeting. We must use our influence and act decisively." He paused and smiled. "Nip it in the bud as President Brown likes to say."

* * * * *

They had been together for three weeks, ten days of which had been spent in a sweaty jungle training camp, and they knew one another now, trusted one another, knew they had been chosen because they were the best.

Before leaving the U.S. Southern Command in Panama, Captain Vazquez, the man who would lead the mission in the jungle, had ordered his troops to turn over their clothing, their dog tags, cigarette lighters, pocket knives, wallets, photographs, anything that could identify them as Americans if they were captured or killed.

Vazquez watched his nine troops line up silently in their new clothes — light weight khaki pants and shirts that would not immediately identify them as soldiers if they were spotted. Their personal belongings lay on a table in clear plastic bags like discarded items at a mortuary — confirmation that their training was over, that this was real.

No one had much to say. Company scout Paulina Holgodo stared at the floor, head down. Radio operator Johnny Mareno fiddled with his rucksack. Medical officer Marta Guzman checked everyone's food and water and handed out a healthy supply of water purification tablets and survival food tabs in case resupply efforts failed and their MRE's — Meals Ready to Eat — ran out. Machine-gunner Robby Rodriguez smoked his last American cigarette before takeoff.

* * * * *

The C-130 Hercules transport plane was eighty miles off the coast of Peru when the co-pilot spotted the Mirage jet fighter. "Jesus, what the hell is that?"

The pilot saw the plane too and immediately reached for the radio. "This is United States Air Force transport Three-Zero. Our flight plan has been cleared with Peruvian officials. We are unarmed. Repeat unarmed."

The response was a warning burst of machine gun fire sprayed at the rear of the unarmed transport.

In back, Captain Vazquez jumped to his feet and came forward. "What the hell is going on?"

"We're under attack," the pilot shouted. "The sonofabitch won't listen to me."

"Make him listen," Vazquez demanded. "I've got nine people back there, all of whom are vital to this operation."

There was another burst and a yelp from the back.

"Shit, we've been hit," the pilot yelled.

Captain Vazquez hurried back to find his medical officer stooped over one of the soldiers. "It's his leg, Captain," Marta Guzman reported. "There's no way he can make the mission now."

"What's happening, Captain?" asked Paulina Holgodo.

"Some fucking Peruvian fighter pilot got his signals crossed. Bastard thinks he's Rambo. Anyone else hurt?"

Up front, the pilot yelled over his radio to the Peruvian air base Commander in the coastal town of Talara. "Talara tower, we are unarmed U.S. military transport three-zero requesting permission to land. We've been hit by a Peruvian fighter jet. Call your fighter off right now or you've got a real big incident on your hands, buddy. We are unarmed. Our flight plan was cleared by your government and we've been attacked without provocation."

"We can't land at Talara," Captain Vazquez shouted at the pilot. "It's a fucking Peruvian military base. I can't unload a bunch of American troops in khaki pants and straw hats that aren't even supposed to be here in the first place."

"I understand your problem, Captain," the pilot answered. "But we're losing pressure pretty fast. If we don't go down in Talara, we go down in the mountains or the jungle."

"What the hell happened?" asked President Brown when his Chief of Staff walked into the Oval office.

"A French-made Peruvian fighter intercepted them near Talara." A slight twitch in one eye, Robert Little answered, "Our pilot says there was no radio contact before shots were fired. A completely unprovoked attack. The Peruvians say it was just a freak accident ... some miscommunication."

"If there's any question," the President said quietly, "that the operation's been compromised, call it off now."

"No one outside the inner circle could possibly know where those troops were heading," Little explained. "And even if someone suspected, the

Peruvian government would use official channels to voice a complaint. They would never try a stunt like this. It was just an accident at the worst possible time."

"How many were hurt?" asked the President.

"One member of the team. But not critically. He'll be flown back to Panama, debriefed, then kept in a maximum security hospital while he heals. The Op is a few hours behind schedule now, but CIA says it's still a go. Should be going in in a couple of hours by helicopter."

"Who's handling the Press?"

"Wilson over at the Pentagon is issuing a full statement now."

The Washington Post — *Talara, Peru — One U.S. airman was injured today when a Peruvian military plane fired on a U.S. Air Force transport plane. The injured crewman was hurt when the C-130 Hercules was struck by machine-gun fire, said Pentagon spokesman Peter Wilson, but the U.S. plane landed safely near the Ecuadorean border. Peru's President offered an immediate apology for the mix-up and promised a thorough investigation.*

The C-130 was en route to participate in routine anti-drug surveillance operations with the Peruvian Air Force, said Wilson.

The identities of the crew members have not been released.

* * * * *

Madison McGuire unbuckled her seat belt when the sign flashed off. The flight attendant, a young, perpetually smiling woman who had practically gushed all over her while taking her drink order, reappeared with a tiny bottle of Remy Martin and a plastic glass with ice.

Madison's cover called for first class accommodations, a fact which pleased her greatly. She was an English botanist, vacationing in Peru — a cover which required no special tools apart from a few trade journals packed in her suitcase which she would casually leave around her hotel room. And as a tourist she would have a great deal of freedom since no one ever expected tourists to behave in a normal or rational way. Greg Abbott had even hauled in a specialist on Madison's last day at the Barn to teach her enough of the trade jargon so that she could bluff her way through a casual conversation on the subject of botany if she were pressed. Her hair had been darkened a shade and she wore brown contact lenses.

The name on her passport was Hilary Anne Pitt, something Greg Abbott had seen as a wonderful bit of clairvoyance on the part of Langley's document forgers because when the background file on Enrique Navarro had finally arrived, it turned out that his English, and now very dead, wife, had been named Hilary. Abbott was convinced that the name would have a subconscious effect on Navarro and that he would immediately feel a kinship with Madison because of it. Madison was not as enthusiastic. That the name on her passport would remind Navarro of a wife who had been killed six months after his marriage brought her no pleasure and did not appear to be an advantage. What she viewed as a hindrance, Abbott saw as a way to expedite or cement the relationship Madison was to develop with Navarro. But controllers and field agents, like salesmen and secretaries, very often view life differently.

She remembered the day Bob had emerged from the computer room with a smile on his face and Navarro's background file in his stubby fingers. "We've got the goods on our boy," he said happily.

Born Enrique Francisco Diaz in nineteen-sixty, Bob read aloud, his beginnings were far from humble. The father was a general, one of the tiny elite that had ruled the country for years. Enrique was ten years old when his father and a group of military leaders ousted President Fernando Belaunde Terry and shipped him off to exile. The country, Bob announced, still reading from official documents, took a major turn at this point. The military leadership began an overhaul of the system, turning large private estates over to co-ops, restricting the media, nationalizing banks and industry, and committing to buy large shipments of Soviet-made military jets and weapons. The ten-year-long experiment failed miserably. The poor, as it turned out, were not the ones who benefited from the land redistribution programs. Nationalized industries nearly collapsed, annual inflation exploded and the country nearly went bankrupt because military spending far exceeded Peru's revenues.

Being the son of a despised general, Enrique had been sent off to college in Frankfurt for his own safety. When the generals had done all the damage they could do and a civilian government was put into place, General Diaz was killed. The circumstances around his death were kept secret. It was no secret, however, that Enrique had hated his father as much as the people of Peru had hated him. He changed his name immediately after his father's death.

Enrique was politically active in college, Bob related, then wondered aloud if there was anyone in the world who had gotten through college without raising a protest banner at least once. It was at this point in the file that Navarro's future wife was mentioned for the first time. Hilary Pym, it said, radical leftist and active member of the Baader-Meinhof/Red Army Faction whose principal targets were NATO personnel and nuclear facilities. The two had apparently met in the back of a police wagon after a political protest outside the Israeli Embassy had turned violent.

"The beginning of a beautiful relationship," Bob said. "And Enrique's formal introduction to organized anti-government movements. Hilary dies in an automobile accident a year later and Enrique disappears for three months. A former friend of his in Frankfurt told one of our interviewers that he wandered around Europe recovering from his wounds. Other unofficial sources indicate that our boy Enrique might have ended up in a terrorist training camp in Lebanon. Wherever he was, he reemerged when his mother passed away. At that point he went home to the family farm. Poor slob.

He's been quiet till now. Guess his sister's death put some wind back in him. They call his group The National Liberation Front."

Madison uncapped the bottle of Remy Martin and filled her plastic glass, remembering the group at the Barn. Typhoid Mary, who had mercifully left only hours after Madison's arrival. John, the shy researcher who was clearly more comfortable in his lab than in the presence of other humans. He had barely uttered a full sentence the entire time, and even then it was clipped and nervous and straight to the point. Bob, the ping-pong champ, who had bet ten dollars that Enrique Navarro would not give Madison a second glance, even if she did manage to find him, and that, he proclaimed, was a long shot. Greg Allen Abbott, the man who would guide her through the mission.

She let her head fall back on the headrest and thought of Dani, remembered the day they had met, the faded jeans, the black boots, the self-assured smile. Dani had stepped out of the car that day and looked at Madison's secluded home with the wonder of someone who had spent far too much time in the city. She had walked up the stone path towards the house, then stopped suddenly and put her guitar case on the ground. She took Madison's face in her hands, laughed, and kissed both cheeks. Madison would have told her she was lovely that day, but she had lost her voice by then.

She remembered the last time they made love, Dani's deep voice whispering encouragements. Dani's hands. She sighed and closed her eyes, unraveling the mysteries of Dani in her mind, picturing Dani's body, Dani's long fingers, wondering if Dani had the same visions.

Several hundred CIA, Army and Air Force pilots had been evaluated for Operation Maxim Two, but only one met the necessary qualifications: Lieutenant Colonel Richard Jones, a former Air Force officer and member of a select group named Task Force 160. Jones had seen action in Vietnam and most recently he had successfully transported Ranger battalions and Delta Force troops under full fire into Grenada and Panama. He had been nicknamed Night Stalker for his fearless feats of aviation during clandestine insertions. Now, Jones was at the throttle of an enormous Pave Low — an Air Force deep penetration special operations helicopter. Modified for night drops, the Pave Low could fly in total darkness thanks to the installation of an infrared radar that displayed on a small screen high resolution pictures of the ground in front of and below the helicopter. The helicopter was also capable of flying at very low altitudes while maintaining a speed of over 150 miles per hour. With its special silencers that suppressed the roar of the tail rotors, this helicopter was one of the quietest in the world.

Next to Jones was his hand-picked navigator, Captain John Summers. In the rear, the insertion team sat on the floor, buckled in for safety. Two Air Force gunners in jungle camouflage stood next to the .30 caliber mini-guns and rocket launchers mounted on each side of the helicopter.

"Hey, Rich," said Captain Summers, cocking his head towards the team. "Did you notice the weapons those kids are carrying? I don't think we're talking about a friendly visit here. Think the Peruvians know about this?" Richard Jones looked at Summers and raised an eyebrow.

"Yeah," Summers said. "Stupid question, huh?"

"One minute," Jones said over the intercom. Captain Vazquez and the rest of the team unstrapped themselves and stood.

Lieutenant Colonel Richard Jones spotted the area that had been chosen from satellite photographs — a small clearing a mile northwest from the banks of the Huallaga River. He looked at Captain Summers who was watching the infrared screen.

"All clear," Summers reported, and Jones took the aircraft down gently until it hovered just a few feet above the ground.

"*Now,*" Jones said, and Captain Vazquez slid open the cargo door.

Paulina Holgodo exited the helicopter first, ran approximately twenty feet and dropped. Positioning her weapon next to her, she slipped on the night vision goggles, getting her first look at the jungle.

She heard the muffled whine of the turbo engines as the helicopter lifted off the ground, heard Captain Vazquez's quiet order to move out, heard her own heart thumping in her ears as she led the squad out of the insertion area, and for just a moment Paulina Holgodo felt more afraid than she ever had in her life. But the feeling passed, quickly replaced by a soldier's exhilaration.

CHAPTER SIX

For a visitor, Lima at night has the uncomfortable ambience of a city at war. After repeated guerrilla attacks, generators run on limited capacity and one part of the city or another is always unlit. On the hills near the airport and surrounding the wealthier suburbs, torches from miles of shanty-towns glitter like runway lights. *Pueblos jovenes,* the government optimistically calls them — young towns.

Madison formulated her first unhappy impressions of the city on her way to the hotel. Traffic jams and honking horns and shouted obscenities at intersections where street lights no longer glowed red or green. The taxi driver, a heavyset man with a baseball cap worn backwards and bloodshot eyes that watched her in the mirror, cursed impatiently and swerved onto a side street. A short cut, he explained tersely, as the taxi turned sharply and plowed down a darkened alley. Madison saw a group of young boys searching a trash bin for leftovers, then got an unpleasant reminder of her gamma globulin immunizations as the taxi bounced back onto the street.

The driver slammed on the brakes and Madison saw a line of police cars in front of a five-story complex of yellowed stone. There was a fire in the lobby; two fire trucks were pulled up near the entrance. The windows had been blown out to the second floor. A bomb, Madison thought, and had her suspicions confirmed when she saw a bomb squad van and dozens of police officers milling about in full riot gear in case there was more to come.

An ambulance was parked just behind the police barricade, back doors open. Outside the empty vehicle the driver chatted casually with a police officer and smoked cigarettes while he waited. The street had narrowed to one lane and two officers made random checks of passing vehicles. Another officer did his best to direct traffic amidst the chaos of onlookers.

"What's the building?" Madison asked in English, then again in Spanish after getting no response.

"The Chamber of Commerce," the driver answered. "Long live the Sendero. It is the second bombing this week."

"You support the Sendero?" Madison asked. "You believe in them?"

The driver adjusted his baseball cap. "In Lima we believe in change by whatever means."

As the taxi crept closer to the building, he told her to roll down her window and have her passport ready. The smell of sulfur and smoke and exhaust fumes filled the cab. A priest wearing black walked beside two attendants carrying a stretcher, and Madison watched the driver knock the fire off his cigarette and put the butt in his pocket before climbing into his ambulance.

An officer motioned for the taxi to move up, stooped over to inspect the passenger, then studied Madison's passport carefully.

"Welcome to Lima," he said, and Madison saw the taxi driver's bloodshot eyes smiling at her in the mirror as he drove away.

The Gran Hotel Bolivar was just one of Lima's fine luxury hotels, but this one had a distinct British flavor. A nice touch by head office, Madison thought, after the front desk inspected her British passport and informed her politely that tea and petit fours were complimentary every afternoon in the rotunda. Miniature Peruvian and British flags sat in pencil cups on either end of the desk, and a plaque mounted in the front gave a lengthy tribute in Spanish to the British who had built railroads across the country during the nineteenth century war for independence and helped further that revolution.

Madison felt a brush at her sleeve and heard a man's voice. He'd be out for a while, he told the clerk without looking at Madison, and when he left there was an attractive Halliburton briefcase sitting on the floor next to her. The gold handle was engraved with the initials H.A.P. — Hilary Anne Pitt.

Shy John had proudly presented it to Madison as a parting gift on her last day at the Barn, and she had wondered how they would deliver it.

A uniformed boy led her to a suite overlooking the Plaza San Martin, the heart of Lima's business district and a popular spot for nighttime entertainment. The walls were stucco, the drapes a heavy dark wine color. The carpet was cream-colored and shadowed from a recent vacuuming. Madison walked into the bedroom while the boy wheeled in her luggage and opened the double window. A band played dance music in the square below and a group of young people gathered round, dancing, flirting. She saw automobiles at the curb unloading well-dressed patrons of the hotel bar downstairs. She saw people in line for a Schwarzenegger movie across the street and people with shopping bags and smooth suntans and smiles returning to the hotel.

A different Lima had raised its ugly head to her in the taxi, a different world entirely. A world of trash bins and bombs and fleeting images of begging children in headlights, a world so far removed from the Lima that entertained itself in the Plaza. Madison tried to shake off the unsettling feeling that her presence here would only contribute to the crisis, tried to put it off to the first night jitters. But a headache fastened itself around her temples like a vise. She drew the curtains and stepped away from the window, eyes closed for a moment to restore calm. Everything is exaggerated in the field, she reminded herself — stress, joy, despair. *Deep breath. Relax.*

The boy was saying something in Spanish. Madison had nearly forgotten he was there. She turned and found him smiling at her.

"Beautiful view," he repeated, and held his hand out for the tip.

Madison placed a generous gratuity in his palm, and, temporarily at least, managed to feel a bit better about herself.

When the boy left, she went about the business of inspecting the briefcase. It had a built-in automatic defense mechanism that sent out several thousand volts of electric current if the combination was incorrectly dialed or the case was forced open. But Madison, like most field agents, had a clear easy memory for numbers, and dialed up the combination without hesitation.

Inside, she found the 9mm Sig Sauer she had requested, snuggled tightly in a foam case with her shoulder holster. In a satin-lined pen box labeled CROSS, there was a gold-plated ink pen with the same initials as those engraved on the briefcase. *One solid push on the clip and it cocks the internal hammer and slips into firing position,* John had told her. *Another and you've discharged it.* The .22 caliber, single shot pen-gun was capable of doing quite a lot of damage at close range. It also wrote beautifully, Madison discovered when she pulled a sheet of hotel stationary from the drawer and scribbled the name Hilary Anne Pitt.

A slot had been made in the case for a narrow eight-inch-long fiber optic tube, called a Fiber Viewer in John's language, and a tiny hand-held viewing screen. One end of the tube sent a picture to the other end and transmitted it to the pocket viewer. Inserted into a keyhole, under a door or bent round a corner, it allowed the user close-up surveillance that John's lot had only dreamt about a few years ago.

Between the foam lining and a thick layer of reinforced Kelvar fabric that made the case bulletproof, John had placed a mini-transmitter and a crystal controlled receiver so that she could communicate in a variety of ways and on any predetermined frequency with her controller. But Madison had learned over the years that hotel rooms were not the place for private conversations. Hotel rooms sometimes had ears of their own. So she clipped the transmitter mic on the inside of her shirt and dropped the receiver in the pocket of her jeans. She slipped a blazer over her shirt and checked the mirror to be sure there wasn't a bulge over the shoulder holster, then found the 35mm camera in one of her bags and hung it round her neck.

"Remember," Abbott had told her, "you're a tourist. You tip too much and carry lots of luggage. Speak English first and wave that British accent of yours like a flag. Take the camera with you everywhere and load up on hotel brochures, maps, anything you can find to look the part. And Madison, try not to look so goddamned competent, would you? We're going for the tourist thing here, okay?"

* * * * *

The first target was a processing center, code-named Ohio, that Paulina and the team had studied on satellite photos during the mission briefing by Lieutenant Wilkes. She checked her compass and continued moving slowly, carefully, alert to any sound not of the jungle. At night noise is the worst enemy, she had always been taught. The snap of a twig under a foot, the rustle of fabric, a cough or a sniff was enough to advertise your presence to an attentive ear.

The team, with Paulina as scout, had covered three miles at a snail's pace since their insertion. They had several hours of darkness left. Before dawn they would eat, clean their weapons, re-supply their canteens from one of the reed-grown channels, and sleep during the day within a mile of their target. After dark they would move in and destroy the processing center.

Paulina stopped and surveyed the area, night vision goggles in place. There was a faint smell she could not identify. Something other than the rotting reeds she had smelled for the last few hours. She raised her hand and signaled for Rodriguez to hold up. The machine gunner then sent the same signal to the rest of the squad.

She was still for several minutes, listening. Something was different. It was the noises she wasn't hearing that alarmed her. *No birds.* Maybe silence was the real enemy in the jungle at night.

And then it flared up in her goggles like a house fire, a bright light moving at some distance away.

Paulina moved quickly behind a sprawling bush and removed the goggles, waiting for several seconds while her eyes adjusted to the dark. Then she saw it again through her binoculars, bobbing like a flare on the water.

"Captain," she whispered into her radio. "Possible contact approximately two hundred meters. One individual with a lantern. He's moving away from us, but there's a strange smell around here. I think we've found a processing center that's not on the map, sir. There's a lot of light coming off an area about four hundred meters up."

"Hold there," the Captain responded. "I'll let you know."

Captain Vazquez motioned for Sergeant Johnny Mareno, and the communications operator hustled up to the front of the line.

"Radio in our location," the Captain told him. "And tell them we've found a mobile processing center. Find out how we proceed."

Johnny Mareno slipped off the small pack that held his equipment and quickly set up the portable satellite dish. The entire package weighed only twelve pounds and was no more than eighteen inches high fully assembled.

"Singer, this is Fox, over. Do you read?" The signal traveled several thousand miles, bounced off a communications satellite somewhere in space and was sent back down to a listening post in Lima. It took a few seconds for the reply to arrive.

"Fox, this is Singer. Reading you clear. Over," answered Harry Carson — the man the team knew only as Lieutenant Wilkes.

Mareno reported their position and explained the situation. The reply came a full five minutes later.

"Fox, this is Singer. Neutralize obstacle and proceed to main objective. Over."

Mareno and Vazquez looked at each other for a moment, then Mareno answered back. "Roger. Copy the neutralize, Singer. Out."

Several hundred miles away sat an old green van, spray painted on the sides with the name of a moving company. It was driven a few streets each day to a new location so as not to attract attention. But the dark color and cheap art work and dirty mud flaps made it deliberately forgettable. No one in Lima's suburbs seemed to notice the extra aerial that nosed its way through the top or the small port holes for lenses that kept an eye on the street. No one noticed that the old moving van was occupied. In fact, no one seemed to notice it at all.

Harry Carson turned from the wall of communications equipment and looked at Greg Allen Abbott who was stretched out on one of the bunks. "First blood," he said soberly. "There's no going back after this."

A moment later they heard a crackle from Abbott's side of the van. Then Madison's voice came through loud and clear. "French, this is Scorpion checking in as requested. Read me, old man? Someone's going to see me talking to myself out here."

Abbott smiled and grabbed a microphone. "Glad you could make it, Scorpion. Welcome to Lima."

"Second time tonight I've heard that," Madison answered. "And frankly it's given me a bit of a headache."

"Everything all right?" Abbott asked.

"No problems so far. Suppose I'd better get busy though. It's been lovely, Frenchy."

"It's French," Abbott said.

"Yes, well, whatever. Out."

Fifteen minutes later Captain Vazquez and the rest of the team caught up to their scout. "Any other activity?" Vazquez asked Paulina.

"No, sir. We going in?"

"That's our orders. You see any problems?"

"Not from here, sir, but I'll need to scout it out."

"Do it."

"Yes, sir," Paulina answered, then turned back to the Captain. "What about civilians, sir?"

"If they're hanging around a processing center, Holgado, they ain't civilians. I'll stay twenty meters back. The rest of you keep a distance of thirty meters behind me. Let's go."

Paulina took a stick of face paint from her pocket and applied the dark green make-up under her eyes, across her cheeks and forehead, then rubbed it over the backs of her hands. In a few moments she was invisible to everyone but Vazquez who watched appreciatively as she moved like a shadow through the dense jungle.

The ground was soft and she took each step cautiously, careful not to sink too far into the spongy reeds and lose her balance. Her silenced H&K MP5 submachine gun was held firmly in front of her. There was a channel close by. She could smell its rotting banks. With each step she surveyed the area from head to ground, careful of booby traps. It wasn't like training, she thought. Tonight she felt a clearness she had never experienced in training. Her mind evaluated the danger, the terrain, the smells and sounds quickly and easily. She was not calm by any means, but she was well-equipped for the job. Her training told her that.

The target lay ahead barely a hundred meters now, a halo of light in her goggles. She heard new sounds — the low murmurs of human voices, an occasional laugh — but she saw no one. When she was within seventy meters, she raised a hand to notify the captain that she had first visual contact.

There were seven of them, Paulina observed. All, with the exception of one man who was crushing coca leaves like grapes in a huge tub, had rifles slung over their shoulders. *No security outside the site. Smoking and talking.* Paulina and the team badly outclassed them. The thought both comforted and sickened her.

She worked her way back to Captain Vazquez. The rest of the team had joined him by now. "Seven of them, sir, at about a hundred meters," she whispered. "Six are armed. AR-15's and a couple of AK's. The seventh is walking around in a tub of leaves."

"Okay people, it's first contact," Vazquez told his team. "We've practiced this a hundred times. Just like we rehearsed, okay? No difference. Key in when you're all in place. Let's hit it."

Paulina Holgado and Johnny Mareno moved in slowly to within fifty meters of the target. Before Paulina removed her goggles she surveyed the area. Machine gunner Robby Rodriguez was setting up his M-16 on its stand. Marta Guzman, the medic, was by his side with a grenade launcher and an M-16 aimed at the target. Captain Vazquez and the rest of the assault element were moving into position.

Paulina nudged Mareno and they both removed their goggles. They inserted the radio earplug into their ears, keyed their radio three times and waited for the response.

Paulina's heart rate quickened even as she told herself to stay calm. Contact was only seconds away now and the tension was mounting.

Suddenly, Johnny Mareno let out an audible gasp next to her. It was enough to alert the armed processors. Their weapons came off their shoulders quickly. Paulina whipped her head around to see what had happened and saw a snake slithering down the tree Mareno had been using for cover.

It happened in a split second, a barrage of bullets coming their way. The processors were shooting towards the sound. Paulina and Marino hit the ground. Then the muzzle flashes from the assault team's M-16's lit up the night. Paulina raised her head and caught a glimpse of the man who had been crushing coca leaves coming out of the tub with an AK-47 in his hands. She let off two rounds. One exploded into his neck. His finger locked on the trigger of his weapon, but his fire went up into the trees as he fell. Mareno took out another man trying to escape the area.

It was over in less than twenty seconds and their ears rang in the sudden silence that followed the deadly assault. Paulina saw two members of the assault element led by Captain Vazquez move into the area and check the dead. The balance of the team was assembling around the target area.

Paulina Holgado and Johnny Mareno joined them there.

One of the men was still alive. He was trying to crawl away, leaving a trail of blood under the leg he dragged behind him. Captain Vazquez let off a single round into the back of his head. Paulina shut her eyes for a moment.

The captain asked Paulina angrily, "What the hell happened up there, Holgado?"

"It was me, sir," Johnny Mareno broke in. "There was a snake on the tree. It spooked me. I'm sorry, sir."

"Sorry's not enough, Mareno. You almost blew the whole assault. Only half the team had keyed in."

"Sorry, sir," Mareno repeated, head down.

The captain took a deep breath. Combat took its toll on everyone. Now the rush of adrenaline had passed and reality was sinking in. He looked at his team. "This is what war looks like, people. We feel sadness now because we're caring, thinking people. But do you think they ever once shed a tear for our kids, for our friends that died from their poison? No way. You just remember that when you look at these bastards. And you remember another thing too. This was a successful assault. We won tonight."

They stood looking silently at the dead. Machine gunner Robby Rodriguez remembered the father whose heart had suddenly stopped after he'd snorted a line of very clean cocaine off the kitchen table. Robby's six-year-old sister had been sitting on her father's lap that day, had watched him die.

Marta Guzman remembered her mother. She'd last seen her when she was thirteen. Johnny Mareno had lost his sister to an overdose. She was fourteen.

They all had their own ghosts, their own reasons for wanting to be part of Maxim Two. Paulina thought of her brothers, of South-Central, of the hopelessness there, the drugs, and for the first time she believed that the problem was not insurmountable.

CHAPTER SEVEN

She made first for the pavement cafe and ordered a *pisco* sour. The waiter had promised it was the greatest in the city, then hovered over her expectantly when she took the first drink. It was sweet, but she put on her best face for his sake and sipped it slowly, studying the store fronts around the business district. The theater was letting out and Madison watched the movie-goers spill into the plaza. They were mostly young, dressed to kill, and putting on their best struts for the crowd.

Friday nights are the same the world over, she thought, and turned her attention to a group of street vendors, push carts crammed side by side against the wall of a closed bank building. They were packing their goods for the night. No one was shopping.

She put some money on the table for the drink and felt a tickle at her arm, the slippery hand of a pickpocket exploring her blazer. She grabbed the wrist and jerked it up to her, then spun around and found herself looking into the frightened eyes of a child. He could not have been more than eight years old. She loosened her grip, but held the wrist.

"Next time ask *before* you take," she told him in Spanish. His wide, scared eyes glared at her defiantly. She could feel him trembling. She took some money from her pocket and stuffed it into his dirty trousers. "Take this to your mother."

"You should not give them money," she heard the waiter say. "It only makes them worse."

Cities too are the same the world over, she thought. She had seen the boy in New York, in London, seen his hunger in Atlanta, seen his desperate face in every city. And the waiter, or the ones like him, were never far behind. So rigid, so afraid of poverty.

She rose and headed across the plaza for the vendors, stopped and bought from an old man a tiny hand-carved wooden doll in bright Andean clothes, then found someone selling only feather dusters and plastic rulers. He was tall, with a mustache and a straw hat, and looked to be in his late twenties. One of the rulers slipped off the cart while he was packing up and when he stepped round to retrieve it Madison noticed that his shoes were expensive.

"I'm looking for an old friend," she told him. He did not look away from his work. "His name is Frank. From Brazil."

At that his head raised in recognition. "Haven't found Navarro yet. Heard he was in Huancayo. Then we heard he was in Lima recruiting. The Sendero attacked his farm, burned the house down. Someone said he was dead." He shrugged. "Who knows, huh?"

Madison's headache was coming back. *"Christ."*

Someone walked by and he busied himself with his rulers and feather dusters. His head was down and to Madison he sounded as if he were talking through gritted teeth. "Listen, lady, I've been in the streets for a fucking week. Okay? I'm doing the best I can and I sure as hell don't need some bitch from Langley —"

"Do something about your shoes," Madison interrupted mildly. "You look like a bloody banker." *Idiot.*

Early the next morning Madison ordered breakfast in her room and studied a map of Lima by the window light while she ate. The power was out. It went out for a few hours each morning, room service had told her apologetically, then sent bread and soft butter and coffee in a thermal pot that had been brewed sometime before the outage.

She leased a car from an agency in the plaza and set out to find her agents buried in Lima, the camera slung over her shoulder like a badge.

She found one of them working in an outdoor fish market near the docks, sorting anchovies in a tub and stinking to high heaven. But he had nothing of value to offer either. At a tearoom in Miraflores called *La Reja,* she drank bottled water and ate a sandwich and watched a group of country-clubbers pile into golf carts outside their hotel. The suburb of Miraflores was a universe away from downtown Lima by the looks of it — a clean, well-groomed community overlooking the Pacific with red tiled homes, elaborate latticework and palm-lined streets. And during the day, you couldn't see the torches from the shanty-towns.

The tearoom was nestled in a first class hotel called Cesar's, and the manager was a woman named Maria, a long-time Company asset who had established her hotel cover years ago and was kept secret from even the Lima station chief. Which in Madison's mind meant that Maria had probably remained unsoiled by the recent turmoil in the agency and the mole who had caused it all.

They met in her office after Madison sent a note in word code via one of the waiters which said only: *I would have called first but Bobby wanted it to be a surprise. It's been so long since college.*

Maria was a graceful woman of fifty with a warm cinnamon blush and red hair. She welcomed Madison like an old friend, then closed the door, slipped into the chair behind her desk and told Madison everything she had heard about Enrique Navarro. Only a few rumors about Navarro's National Liberation Front had made it as far as Lima, and most of what she had heard came from informants in the *barriadas.* Word travels fast in the shanty-towns, she said, where hope is so desperately needed.

"The people of the new *barriadas* have come from the countryside, have been forced to flee their homes and farms in fear of the guerrillas. They bring with them rumors of a new movement, a new leader who is not afraid to fight. The Sendero made an error in judgment when they attacked Navarro's home in Quinches. Now the people love him even more for what he has lost."

"Someone said Navarro might have been killed in the attack. Have you heard?"

Maria smiled and reached for a silver cigarette case on her desk. "That's what the Sendero wants everyone to believe. But my sources say Navarro knew the attack was coming and escaped in time."

"Do you know where he is now?" Madison asked.

Maria shook her head. "Go to Huancayo where his brother-in-law lives. If anyone can get a message to him it will be Jose Muro." She opened the cigarette case and withdrew a small piece of paper. "Here's the number of a trustworthy guide. You'll need him. Many of the roads are not marked properly. He knows the mountains."

Anthony the guide was a cheerful man who took a liking to Madison right off when she conveyed her instructions in fluent Spanish and offered him a fair price without haggling. She told him she was a botanist on vacation and before they were out of the city made him stop for a small shovel and some cardboard boxes where she could put samples in case they happened across something interesting.

In less than an hour the ear-popping ascent into the great Andes began and the highway turned into a snaking one-lane dirt track of blind mountain curves. White crosses marked places where travelers had misjudged the turns and plunged into the breathtaking Andean chasm.

The Toyota Land Cruiser took the narrow mountain roads at a crawl. Four hours into the hundred-mile trip they reached fifteen thousand feet, and Madison was in the early stages of *soroche*. He covered her with a blanket when the altitude sickness brought on chills, and made her keep it on even when the sweat was pouring from her hairline. Her fever shot up and her words were no longer intelligible, but it was too late for Anthony to turn back — Huancayo was only twenty miles away and Madison needed attention.

She woke naked in sweat-soaked sheets with Anthony sitting at her bedside. "Drink this," he said. "It will help."

"Where are we?" she asked. It had taken only a few minutes for her color to return. Anthony refilled her cup. The room was dark and small and cool. One window was covered with a hand-woven blanket and a soft yellow light was seeping through. She heard dogs barking somewhere in the distance.

"Huancayo," he answered. "I am sorry about the room, but the *soroche* didn't want to wait for better accommodations. I had to carry you inside."

"Thank you."

"You must sleep. I'll be over there." He pointed to a chair in the corner and shrugged. "This I apologize for also, but I could not afford two rooms."

Madison glanced at the pile of clothes she had worn on the floor. Next to it was her briefcase and the small bag she had brought with her.

"You are worried about this, I think," he said, and handed her the 9mm Sig.

Madison popped out the clip and checked it. *Full.*

Anthony looked at the gun in her hands, then withdrew quietly to his chair. Madison watched him fold his arms across his chest and close his eyes. He was dark-skinned with dark hair and eyes and a day's worth of beard. He had on a dingy white undershirt and the roll around his waist overlapped his belt.

"Do you have family, Anthony?"

He opened his eyes and smiled. "A wife, a lazy brother and one beautiful daughter who is now fourteen and thinks I am very stupid."

She smiled and nodded. "What was in the tea?"

"Coca leaves," he said with a chuckle.

Slightly anesthetized, Madison sank into a restless sleep and nightmares of surly teenage girls planting white crosses just outside the window.

Sleeping in the jungle during the day was not easy. The nights were cooler this time of year in Peru, but the daytime temperatures were very high, and their filthy heat-soaked khakis clung to their backs when they emerged from under the brush they had used for cover. The bugs were another problem, apparently undeterred by the commercial repellent they had sprayed themselves with before going belly-up for the day.

They woke at dusk to the medic, Marta Guzman, checking canteens and forcing each soldier to drink a full quart of water. No one wanted water, but they all drank, knowing they had lost vital fluids all day in their sleep. Next came the MRE's which no one wanted either, but they ate because they knew the food would convert to much needed energy later.

Robby Rodriguez sat with Paulina while they ate. "Man, we took them out last night, didn't we?" He laughed and shook his head. "I was scared shitless. I just kept thinking, man, this is real combat and you don't know shit."

Paulina nodded. "Me too. I never really thought we'd be here, you know? I don't know. You think we're doing the right thing?"

Rodriguez finished his food, red beans and rice, and poked at the ground with a stick. "Ain't our call. We just follow orders the best we can and count on the higher ups to know what's best. We got the easy job when you think about it."

"Yeah. I guess."

He stood and gathered up his trash. They would find a spot to bury all their waste before they left the area. "Just wish I had a beer."

"Yeah," Paulina answered.

The site called Ohio was less than a mile from where they had camped, no more than a tiny clearing on the satellite map. But to get there they would have to cross through a small village.

Paulina was especially cautious now in case any of the locals hunted the jungle, taking each step carefully and surveying the area before taking another. Time was unimportant at this point. Caution was the key. The rest of the squad stayed well behind and only spoke when absolutely necessary and then only in Spanish or Quechua.

Paulina keyed her radio twice in a prearranged signal to let Rodriguez know she was approaching the village. The machine gunner held up his hand to let Vazquez and the rest of the team know it was time to stop and wait for word from their scout.

It wasn't much of a village, a few reed huts built in a circle and a couple of torches burning in the center. A path big enough for a vehicle was beaten down around the small community, but Paulina saw no vehicles. Two women, topless and brown, sat outside a hut and worked under the light of a torch. They were laughing and binding reeds and grass around the frame of a boat. Paulina watched them for a few minutes. One of them looked pregnant.

She circled round the village and heard a baby crying in one of the huts. A woman sang to it softly.

Where are the men?

She circled back and found Captain Vazquez. "The village is tiny. Three women. No men. We can go around on the east side without any contact."

Vazquez nodded. "Keep your eyes open when we get past the village."

When Paulina was in visual range of Ohio, she understood why she had seen no men in the village. Through her binoculars she saw five of them, local natives with no shirts. Two men crushed coca leaves in two large tubs. One poured liquid from glass bottles into the tubs. Probably the acid they used to turn the leaves to paste, Paulina thought. The other two men unloaded jute bags from a farm truck.

The center was surrounded by twelve armed guards. No one was smoking or drinking or talking tonight. Half of the guards were facing away from the workers, alert eyes on the jungle, AR-15's held with both hands across their chests. *They've heard about the attack last night.*

She had replaced the binoculars with her night vision goggles and turned to start back. Then, the rustle of branches. She whipped her head around and saw the figure moving towards her at fifty meters. *They've sent out a scout.*

In the pitch dark without night vision equipment the naked eye only detects movement, so Paulina held perfectly still, feeling the pulse in her neck throbbing against her shirt collar. The figure was heading back towards the camp, and Paulina was directly in his path.

The figure stopped. It was a man, Paulina saw now, and he had a rifle slung over his shoulder. He paused and looked around as if he sensed being watched. Paulina used the time to remove her goggles and crouch behind a tree, her silenced MP5 held in position.

She got her vision back when he was within thirty meters, nothing more than a black outline in the night without the goggles. His approach had slowed but he was still heading straight for her.

Twenty meters. Paulina slipped the selector switch to the single shot firing position.

She aimed at the center of the forehead.

Ten meters. She squeezed the trigger and heard

the muted crack from her silenced submachine gun, heard his rifle fall into the bush.

Target down.

Her first sensation was something that came with extensive training and strong survival instincts — pure exhilaration at a successful assault. She sprang forward, MP5 held steady on the target, and kicked the fallen rifle out of reach. With her night vision goggles back in place, she evaluated the damage. Her aim had been off slightly and the bullet had hit just below the ear. The subject had no pulse.

And then she saw what she had not seen in the distance. He wore old gym shorts, no shirt, no shoes. She ran a hand along the bottom of one foot. It was hard and calloused. *Jesus, I've killed one of the villagers.*

She remembered the briefing. No contact with locals, Lieutenant Wilkes had told them. If they see you, you'll have to neutralize them. Word spreads fast in the jungle.

She collected his rifle and concealed it under some brush, then followed the same routine with the body before heading back to the squad.

By the time Paulina found Captain Vazquez and the others she had calmed down considerably, had done what every soldier must do at one time or another — rationalize. She had had no choice, she told herself. She had acted according to training, had responded correctly, had passed the true test of combat. And this man, this local native was carrying a gun, was heading for the objective, *was* the enemy. She wrapped that rationale around her like a warm blanket, finding in it the strength she must have to continue the mission. To stop now — to question —

meant failure, and she knew it was too late to turn back.

"There's twelve armed guards, sir, and four natives doing the work. One vehicle. They had a scout, but he's been neutralized, sir." She didn't elaborate.

Paulina and Johnny went in first while the rest of the assault team flanked them slightly and spread out around the perimeter of the processing site. Paulina heard the rumble of an engine and keyed her radio five times. Captain Vazquez keyed back twice to let her know he had heard it too. Another farm truck pulled up. The driver got out with a passenger and together they dropped the wooden sides of the truck. Two more men piled out of the back with rifles, followed by two more workers. The workers began unloading more bags.

"That's poison that'll never make it to the States," Johnny Mareno whispered.

"There's eighteen of them now," Paulina muttered more to herself than to Mareno. "Won't be as easy as last night."

One of the armed guards left his position and walked to the truck. Paulina assumed he was in charge when he ordered the two armed men who had come from the back of the truck out into the jungle as lookouts.

Paulina keyed her radio five times. *Danger.* The Captain responded as before, and Paulina hoped that whatever he had planned for the two sentries would happen quietly.

Then came a shout and a burst of automatic weapons fire, and everything came apart at once. The workers were running. The armed guards opened up and fired wildly at the tree line. Johnny Mareno took a round in the chest and went down with an angry growl. Paulina dropped to check his condition and heard the metallic pops from the assault team's M-16's battering the objective. When she rose, two guards at about seventy meters were working their way deeper into the tree line, slipping through a gap left by the assault element.

She grabbed her MP5 and went after them. Away from the tracers and the bright lanterns around the processing site, the jungle seemed to absorb the two men. She slipped on her goggles and studied the area through the green display.

Noise. She rotated her head slightly to the right and saw him. He was behind a tree, the rifle raised.

Shit. She threw herself to the ground as he fired, ripping off the night vision goggles as she rolled. She lost sight of him in the sudden darkness and it sent a wave of panic rushing through her. Then she heard him running, saw his dark outline darting through the trees. She switched the selector switch to burst and fired into his back. He took several rounds before he dropped.

She returned the goggles and switched on the display. She stood there silently for several minutes, listening, looking for any movement, any trace of the other man. *Nothing.* He had vanished.

By the time she returned to the objective, the assault team had moved in and Captain Vazquez was counting bodies. "We've got two missing."

"I got one, sir," Paulina said, still trying to catch her breath. "The other got away. Captain . . . Johnny's dead."

The bodies were lined up. Captain Vazquez found Mareno's body, stripped it and collected his gear. It was something he could not ask his soldiers to do.

The huge wooden tubs were dismantled and thrown onto the trucks where other team members were dumping the bags of coca leaves. Robby Rodriguez and Marta Guzman stuffed gasoline soaked rags into the gas tanks and lit them.

The team moved out without a word. No one knew what to say.

On a hilltop in Lima, Harry Carson sat in the old van studying one of the satellite charts pinned to the wall. His insertion team had made all their checkpoints within the expected time, even when they had dealt with the unexpected. He traced his finger along a line of jungle on his map. Ohio was highlighted in yellow. They should be there by now, he thought.

"Singer, this is Fox. Over."

Carson turned back to the racks of equipment and lifted his mic. The voice was female. *Where's Mareno?* "This is Singer. Go ahead, Fox. Over."

"Ohio has been neutralized, Singer. Fox reporting one casualty. Repeat. One casualty. Mareno. Over."

It took Carson a few seconds to respond, but he gave them their orders and the location of the next target, an airstrip code-named Phoenix four miles up the banks of the river.

Greg Abbott's attention had been drawn by the call and he crossed the van and sat next to Carson.

"Lost one of ours," Carson said quietly. "One of theirs got away. *Damn.* Those poor kids must be scared shitless."

CHAPTER EIGHT

The sound of church bells echoed through the valley, calling Huancayo's faithful to worship. They emerged from their homes, hundreds of them. Madison watched their pious climb to the mountain church from the motel manager's front porch, watched them in their bright Sunday best making their way into the hills like sleepless shadows at dawn. An occasional army Jeep full of soldiers roared past.

The manager gave Madison and Anthony black coffee and fried potatoes and let them use his sink to freshen up because there were no baths in the rooms. Madison asked him about the soldiers and he told her that Huancayo had been officially classified an emergency zone since the attack on the agricultural co-op, and the soldiers kept a high visibility in hopes of discouraging further guerrilla violence.

"But I put no faith in the army. The government does not care about the interior, only about Lima and the coast. The soldiers will be gone in a few days. My daughter is fourteen. She had never seen an army soldier until the attack. Sometimes here in the interior, the Sendero is the only authority we know."

Madison asked if he supported the Shining Path, asked if he believed in their "destroy in order to reconstruct" philosophy. He pointed to the jail down the hill.

"There are three guerrillas being held in our jail. They hold a sign out the window when people pass. It says that the revolution is not destroyed by blood, the revolution flourishes in blood. What man is brave enough to stand up and declare that he does not support them?"

"I hear that there is such a man," Madison said. "A man called Navarro. Heard of him?"

But her frankness had frightened him and he refused further discussion on the subject. They finished their coffee quietly.

On the other side of Huancayo, they passed a girl carrying her shoe shine trade in a battered suitcase. She wore coveralls and looked to be about twelve years old. She was taking her business to a large fair in the mountains, Anthony explained, and her trade today may feed the family next week. Madison could not remember exactly what her own concerns had been at age twelve, but she was sure it was nothing so grave. And just when she was sinking into depression again, the girl stuck out her tongue at them and slapped at the side of the Toyota as they passed.

Anthony honked the horn and roared with laughter. "Kids today, huh?"

They found a group of small houses, but there were no numbers so they had to ask around to find the address. A man without a shirt answered the door and seemed startled at seeing an unfamiliar face. He sucked in his gut and rubbed the sleep from his eyes. He had not been awake for long.

"Good morning." Madison smiled. "Jose Muro?"

"Yes," he answered, but his eyes were suspicious and he glanced over his shoulder once quickly.

Madison heard a hollow thump from inside the house and knew he was not alone. "May I come in for a moment, please?" she asked.

Jose Muro scanned the area behind Madison. His eyes widened when he saw Anthony sitting in the Toyota. "My guide," she explained. "I'm not from here. England actually. Sorry to bother you so dreadfully early but it really *is* important."

Muro smoothed his hair and stepped away from the door. "My English is not good," he said, and directed her to an unfinished wooden table in the living area.

There were two half-full coffee cups on the table and Madison casually pushed one aside as she sat down. *Still warm.* A worn boot lay next to a closed bedroom door and Madison realized that the sound she had heard from the door had been the thud of a single boot falling on the wood floor.

"I'm looking for Enrique Navarro," Madison said in Spanish. But Jose merely shrugged. "Your brother-in-law. I'd like to see him."

"I have not seen Enrique for some time."

"I have a message for him from an old college friend," Madison said. "Tell him it's from Fritz, would you?" She withdrew her passport from the back pocket of her jeans and let it drop open on the table. "My name is Hilary Pitt. I'll be in Lima at the Gran Bolivar."

Jose checked the photograph and the name on the passport. "I do not expect to see him."

Madison made for the door, then turned. "Tell your brother-in-law he needs new boots. Good day, Señor Muro."

"Two of my processing sites in two days," Julio Bermudez roared, and slapped the top of his desk in frustration. "Hundreds of pounds of product destroyed. It is a slap in my face. If that idiot pilot had known what he was doing, we would not have these problems. They would all be dead. It was a cargo plane. What's so hard about shooting down a cargo plane?" He looked up at his security chief, who was standing in front of the desk, and frowned. "And you stand there grinning at me like an imbecile. Where have you been?"

"I have been collecting valuable Intelligence, Julio," his head of security said dutifully. He always bowed slightly when he addressed his boss. "We have a survivor from one of the raids. I had him flown here and interrogated fully. I think you will find the results of the interrogation interesting." He dropped a stack of papers on Bermudez's desk. "We now know how many Americans we are dealing with, what direction they are heading and what kind of weapons they are using. We also have pictures of the two processing sites after the raids were carried out."

Bermudez began reading the report. "Only eight of them now. The commander at Talara said nine walked off the C-130. They have lost a soldier it seems." He smiled. "And how long before they have to be resupplied?"

"Only a few days, Julio."

Bermudez looked at the report again. "How did this man escape?"

The security chief smiled. "He never left the site. He buried himself under the brush a few yards away. One of the soldiers ran right overtop of him during the confusion."

Bermudez nodded and gestured for him to sit. "You have a recommendation?"

The security chief took the chair closest to Bermudez's desk. "The area is under Sendero control. They have promised us protection and freedom to run our operations for part of the profits. If they saturate the area with troops it would only be a matter of time before the Americans are found. Also, with Sendero forces in the jungle, helicopter resupply efforts would be hampered. Eventually they will run out of food and ammunition."

Julio Bermudez thought it over. "Yes. It's an option we will consider. But first, let's amuse ourselves with President Brown for a while. I have a journalist friend in Managua who will be very interested to know about the latest U.S. aggression against a poor nation. After our fun, we will let the Sendero end it swiftly and decisively."

She could see nothing for miles but the snow-capped peaks of the Andes and the velvety dark green carpet that covered the jagged foothills. In daylight, it was the most dazzling country Madison had ever seen.

They passed a colonial-era church that sat in a meadow of grazing sheep. "A nice ride without *soroche*, huh?" Anthony said, smiling. "In the earthquakes of eighty-one, the village was destroyed but the church stood. The religious leaders said the end of the world was coming. But Peru still stands too."

They had passed through Quinches and covered another two miles of road, climbing higher into the Andes before the descent to Lima would begin. Madison watched out the window, let the thin, clean air fill her lungs, let her mind wander. She wasn't sure if Navarro had been in Muro's house, but she felt sure Navarro would get her message. She had done everything possible to let his brother-in-law know that she was not a threat. She had shown her passport willingly, had made it clear that she believed Navarro was in the house, but that she would wait for him to come to her on his terms. And he would come, she was convinced of that. The name she had used, and the name of Fritz, would stir his curiosity. She had remembered the name from Navarro's background file. Fritz had been the best man at Navarro's wedding, a close friend to both Enrique and Hilary.

Madison closed her eyes and leaned her head back. Huancayo had been a success, a tiny step in the right direction, the first small victory since her arrival. The next move belonged to Navarro. And now came the hardest part. The inactivity, the waiting. But then that's what her career had been till now, she mused, that's what spying was — dreadful inertia mixed with bouts of frenzy. And now the track had been laid and the rollercoaster ride had begun in earnest.

She was drifting off when she felt Anthony brake, felt Anthony's hand brush her knee. She opened her eyes to see a paneled farm truck blocking the road a quarter mile ahead, and then she saw the tension on Anthony's face. "A roadblock," he said nervously.

"The Sendero hasn't come this far yet," Madison said, studying the truck.

Anthony shook his head. "They have not taken any of the countryside in this area. But they sometimes set roadblocks as a small reminder of their power. A reminder that they are moving towards the cities." He slowed even more and turned to Madison. "You must tell me the truth now, before we reach them. Is there any reason the Sendero would be looking for you?"

"No," Madison answered.

Anthony looked at her for a moment. "I dearly hope you are telling the truth. If you are lying, you will have to be fast with that gun you carry."

Every field agent in the world, from Lebanon to Beijing, has heard stories of what happens to suspected spies at roadblocks. Some agents carry concealed weapons for protection. Some carry cyanide because the story goes that if they take you, by the end of the first night you will gladly turn in your best friend. And all agents looking in the face of a roadblock find themselves mistrusting everything and everyone, wondering if Langley's document forgers are really the best in the world, wondering if their passport will hold up to scrutiny, wondering if they've been blown, wondering if an agent has turned.

Madison checked the clip in the 9mm and slipped the pen gun into her palm. Anthony glanced at her but said nothing.

They were within thirty yards and still the truck had not moved. The Toyota was crawling forward in first gear and Madison saw the outline of two faces in the cab of the truck. From behind came the growl of another engine. Anthony checked his rearview mirror and cursed.

"There's another truck behind us. Don't turn around."

"How many in the cab?" Madison asked, sticking the 9mm in the back of her jeans.

"One," he answered. "Maybe some in the back also, but I cannot see." He shouted out his window to the truck blocking the road. "You broken down? Need some help?" He whispered for Madison to stay in the car, then opened the driver's door and stepped out.

Two figures emerged from the front truck, one male, one female, AK-47's pointed at Anthony.

Madison heard a door slam behind her and saw in her side mirror a man climb out of the cab of the second truck.

Anthony had his hands in the air. He was smiling and shuffling, trying to make jokes. Madison heard him say he had been hired to show her the countryside, that he made his living off rich women.

Then she heard the unmistakable sound of a rifle click into firing position next to her. She turned her head slowly and saw the AK pointed at her temple.

The two from the first truck had searched Anthony and were heading for the Toyota. From behind, Anthony was yelling to them that Madison did not understand Spanish.

"Get out." The man with the AK pointed at her head spoke in Spanish. "Get out," he repeated, but Madison merely shrugged as if she didn't understand, grateful to Anthony's quick thinking. It had bought her some time.

They came towards her slowly, the man stopping in front of the vehicle, the woman looking directly into Madison's eyes as she approached. She was young and sure of herself, with grey eyes as hard as granite.

"Could be the American spy," said one of the men in Spanish. "If the passport is British we must question them carefully."

The woman came around and stood next to Madison's door. "Papers," she said in clear English, and Madison made a show of searching for her passport while she checked the positions of the two men. Anthony stood near the roadblock looking at her helplessly. One man leaned on the front of the Toyota with his rifle slung over his shoulder, watching Anthony. Another stood next to the woman, rifle held steady and ready to fire.

"Ah, then, here it is," Madison said cheerfully, smiling at the woman. "Thought I'd lost it. Didn't expect to be stopped, actually. But one never knows when —"

"Give it to me," the woman interrupted.

Madison leaned out the window slightly, passport in hand. When the woman reached out for it, she took one step in front of the gunman and Madison rammed an elbow into her solar plexus, then brought a back fist up against the bridge of her nose. She heard the crack, felt the bone give. The force of the blow knocked the woman backwards and Madison kicked the door open, slammed it into the gunman and discharged the single-shot pen gun into his chest.

She rolled out of the vehicle and saw Anthony jump the other man from behind before he could get the AK-47 free. Anthony pulled the rifle off his shoulder and tried to wrestle him to the ground. But he was strong and Anthony couldn't bring him down. Madison came around and delivered a punishing front kick, plunging the ball of her foot between his legs. He fell to his knees and Anthony tumbled off his back.

"Get the gun," Madison yelled, but Anthony wasn't fast enough and the guerrilla got to it first. She fired a single shot from the 9mm into his thigh, but the AK-47 was still coming up in her direction. She aimed the next shot at the center of his forehead and hit the mark.

Anthony was lying on his back, hands on his chest, gasping for breath. Madison held out a hand

CHAPTER NINE

ert Little tucked his briefing papers inside a
and made his way up the corridor towards the
House West Wing. He passed through the
detectors as he had done on a hundred
gs and found the usual group of Secret
on hand outside the Oval office, beige
es coiling up from their jackets, handguns
at their sides.

esident in yet?" he asked one of the agents.

e's with someone."

e Chief of Staff was not accustomed to waiting,

for him. "Up you go, old man. Work to do." She
went back to the Toyota and found her passport
lying on the ground.

Anthony came around to survey the damage. He
looked at the woman's face covered in blood, then
saw the man with the .22 caliber hole in his chest.
He muttered something inaudible.

Madison dragged the woman back to the second
truck. She was breathing but unconscious. Anthony
picked up the woman's feet and helped Madison stuff
her into the cab of the truck. "Let's get those two
into the other truck," Madison said, pointing at the
bodies of the two men. "Put it in neutral. We'll roll
it off. Think there's more Sendero in the area?"

"The only thing I am sure of," he answered, "is
that you are not a botanist."

They loaded the men's bodies into the back of the
farm truck and Anthony slipped it into gear and
moved it to the edge of the drop-off. He jumped out
of the truck and Madison climbed into the driver's
seat of Anthony's Toyota. She eased it forward until
the bumpers made contact. A few moments later
they watched the farm truck tumble into the Andean
abyss.

"If you let that woman live," Anthony said, "the
Sendero will find out about you. You will make an
enemy of them." There was something in his voice
that Madison had not heard before. It was the
decisiveness of a man who had learned to evaluate
risks.

She stopped and turned. "Who are you?"

"The best guide in the country." He shrugged. "I
also work for your agent Maria from the hotel. For
six years now."

"You might have blown us both sky high," Madison snapped angrily.

"I assure you, I am not a *known* informant. Maria keeps my identity from even your agency. I don't even know anyone else in your business. Maria called and asked that I take special care of you, said you were an associate," Anthony explained, trailing Madison back to the Land Cruiser. "And it is a good thing I was here when you got the altitude sickness, hey?" He touched her shoulder and waited for her to turn, then spoke quietly, seriously. "It is very dangerous to leave that woman alive."

Madison turned back to him slowly. Oh, how well you've learned the trade, she thought. But he was right. The woman could identify her, could jeopardize the entire operation. How many times have I sold my soul for the greater good, she asked herself, and closed her eyes for a moment before starting towards the truck where they had left the unconscious guerrilla.

The cab of the truck was empty. She was gone. *Christ.*

Those who knew Madison McGuire best had grown accustomed to her long silences, but Anthony knew her barely, and her quiet on the trip back disturbed him greatly. And so, to punish her, he delved into his own thoughts as she had delved into hers, and drank steadily from a whiskey bottle hidden under the seat.

While Anthony sulked, Madison went over her first encounter with the Sendero. She thought of the woman who had gotten
was her own critical la
allowed it to happen. And
great deal of amazement t
one but Dani Stone du
Through it all, somewher
preservation, there had bee
her mind like a beacon in

She thought of all the
her job over the years. In t
more of a calling than a c
others did it, because h
because nothing else inspire
exhilaration.

A Korean *Tae Kwon Do*
that one learns great things
routinely faces death. Youn
spent the next year work
herself half to death every
know herself better. In the
that fear was relative, that
less threatening when one h
a Mac-10, and that submach
notch when you've slept in Be
rocked the city.

The more experienced M
reasons for continuing her w
select, to be rooted more in c
discovery or thrill or anger. B
it for Dani.

Ro
folder
White
metal
morni
Servic
earpie
bulgir
"P
"H
T

had never been asked to wait to see the President. Little himself scheduled all of the President's appointments personally, was aware of everyone who stepped into the Oval office and what business they wanted to discuss. Everyone knew the rules. Everyone was required to brief the Chief of Staff fully before he would agree to schedule an appointment with the President. Until now. Had the rules changed? Or had someone simply maneuvered his way past him in yet another Washington power play?

The door of the Oval office opened. The Secret Service agents, the President's secretary, and his special assistant jumped to their feet.

The President stepped out, a fit man of sixty-four, with hazel eyes and coarse graying hair. Through the door the Chief of Staff glimpsed Mitchell Colby, the Director of Central Intelligence. Little ran a finger over the lid of his left eye to try and control the spasm.

"Come in," President Brown said to Little, then turned to the head of his Secret Service detail. "Have someone send in coffee." He sat down behind the desk that had been an Oval Office fixture since the eighteen hundreds and pushed aside a stack of position papers to make room for his elbows.

Little nodded curtly to Colby upon entering the Oval Office, then joined the DCI across the desk from the President.

"Show him what you've got," the President said.

Colby withdrew a single sheet of paper from a folder and handed it to Little. "It's going to show up in print in *Barricada* later today. Complete with the photographs," Director Colby added.

Little studied the sheet. "Oh, God," he muttered. "How the hell? It's not even accurate. They've exaggerated the number of soldiers we ... Where did this come from?"

"We picked it up on the wire service this morning," Director Colby answered. "It's a leftist paper from Managua. It routinely launches this kind of attack on U.S. policy."

The President broke in. His voice was controlled but Robert Little knew him well enough to know he was angry. "It says that we've begun a genocidal attack against Peru's peasants and to prove it they're including pictures of the dismantled processing sites. Damn it, Bob. Why haven't you kept me briefed? I didn't know one of the processors had escaped. I didn't even know one of our boys was killed."

Little glanced at Colby. "CIA only told me yesterday, Mr. President. I was going to brief you this morning but I see Mitch beat me to it."

"My people woke me at three a.m. with this wire report," Colby explained calmly. "I thought the President should know immediately."

The steward knocked lightly and appeared with a tray of coffee. The men were silent while he filled their cups.

"The question is, gentlemen," said President Brown when the young man had left through a side door, "what kind of damage control is needed?"

"We've already released the outline of the Andean Initiative to the Press," Little answered confidently. "We've been up front with the American people.

They support a military program to slow the flow of drugs into this country. This is not another secret war in the jungle no matter what that paper says."

"Yes," Colby added calmly. "But no one knows those soldiers are in there yet. That includes Congress, I might add. The operation has been kept entirely on a need to know basis so far."

"It's simple," Little said. "We deny the article and the photographs. I assure you, Mr. President, a leftist paper from Managua will have no credibility with anyone in this country."

"I hope you're right," Colby said, rubbing his scruffy chin. "Frankly, Mr. President, my concern is the insertion team. They're fair game now. If the drug lords decide we're doing too much damage they can send in their own troops. Hell, they can send for the Sendero if they want. They all share the same business interest. They're all connected. I say we extract the jungle team now. We can have them home for debriefing in a day."

"And what about the Andean Initiative?" the Chief of Staff demanded. "The war on drugs gets too tough so we pull out? We have to consider the election. We're hitting them where it hurts and they're fighting back through the Press. That's all."

Colby shook his head. "I say we pull out now before this thing blows up in our faces."

The President sighed and walked to the thick bullet-resistant windows that looked out onto the White House lawn. He spoke without turning around. "I need some time to think it over."

Colby and Little stood. "Mr. President," the Chief

of Staff said. "I've been a trusted advisor in this administration for over three years. I've never led you astray. Trust me on this, sir."

"We'll talk later, Bob." The President still had not turned around.

In the corridor outside the Oval office, Robert Little caught up with Colby. "Don't ever go over my head again, Mitch. Ever."

The old Director smiled and kept walking at a good pace. "Your insecurity is showing, Robert."

Robert Little put a firm hand on Colby's shoulder. "Better learn who your friends are."

Mitchell Colby stopped and rotated his head until he was looking at the hand on his shoulder. He cocked one bushy eyebrow and raised his eyes slowly to the Chief of Staff. "Let me tell you something. I'm old and I'm on my way out anyway, and I don't give a damn about re-election politics. If you dick around and get my people killed, I'm going to have a hell of a story to tell before I leave."

A look of pure astonishment crossed Robert Little's face. "Are you threatening me?"

Colby checked the corridor in both directions. "You do the right thing, Robert, or I'll hang you out to dry."

Captain Vazquez and Paulina Holgodo watched Phoenix through binoculars as three men loaded boxes into a private plane. The landing strip was lit with a line of small torches for pilot visibility.

"One grenade from Marta's launcher would take care of it, Captain," Paulina noted. The death of the communications sergeant had only served to strengthen the resolve of the team.

"Orders are no contact," Vazquez answered, still watching the objective.

Paulina nodded. "We've had enough excitement, I guess."

"Can you read the tail numbers?" Vazquez asked.

"Just barely, sir, but I got them."

"Get Marta up here with the radio."

"Singer, this is Fox. Do you copy? Over," said medic Marta Guzman who now had the added duty of communications since Johnny Mareno had been killed.

Harry Carson turned to his equipment and grabbed the microphone. "Fox, this is Singer. Copy you loud and clear. Go ahead, over."

"We've made Phoenix, sir. There's activity. Three men loading a Beechcraft King Air with boxes. It's a four-passenger aircraft. Probably holds a lot of product." Guzman reported the tail number to Carson. "Looks like they're preparing for takeoff, sir. We've got two pilots climbing in now. Over."

"What's the security like around Phoenix? Over." Carson looked at the spot on his map where the insertion team was now positioned.

"Total of four individuals and one Jeep not counting the pilots. A supply shack just like it showed on the satellite photos, but we haven't had time to check it out ... Okay, sir, engines have started. It's about to fly. Over."

"Roger that. Hold your position and maintain surveillance. Good work, Fox. Singer out."

Carson turned to the computer keyboard and typed in a high priority code followed by his report and the Beechcraft's tail number.

The report would be decoded at CIA headquarters in Langley, then passed on to the Drug Enforcement Administration and Coast Guard. If the plane was headed for the States, it was in for quite a welcome.

Carson smiled. "Now, that's the way it should be done."

There is not a creature in the world more aware of its surroundings than a field agent whose cover's been blown, and as Madison picked her way through the back streets of Lima, she kept a careful eye.

The evening was cool. Peru's winter was only a month away, and as a reminder gray-white clouds hung low over the jammed rooftops. The smells from food stalls and apartments wafted past her in a heavy fog bank the locals called *garua* — steaming chicken livers and skewers of beef heart, orange, and mint, all mixed together. And the sounds of Lima — melodies from Andean harps, crying, singing, cooking, bargaining, beggars and tire changers shouting to traffic.

She turned into an alley and saw two women standing motionless at a doorway. She heard them whisper as she passed and suddenly she was acutely aware of being an intruder. The Americans have come, she thought. We're here to save you whether you want to be saved or not. And after we've disregarded your culture and pressed our wishes on you, we'll want you to love us for it. That's our way. But we do it with the very best of intentions.

She spotted the building she had been looking for and entered without looking back. Greg Abbott had given her the address when she returned from Huancayo. They both knew it was only a matter of time before the Sendero posted watchers in Lima and spotted Madison. "Huxley's the best forger in town," he had told her. "He'll fix you up. Has a partner named Cheri. A little out of it but she does good work."

The staircase was dark and smelled of souring food. Madison tugged at the string on a bare bulb. It gave one brilliant flash then burned itself out, leaving her to grope her way up two levels. She knocked at the door and saw a shadow shade the peephole. "It's Hilary," she said. "French told me to stop in."

The door opened and a scrawny cat pressed by. A woman in a pale blue frock and too much makeup called after it then blushed in response to Madison's greeting. Her mouth was turned down in an expression of permanent disappointment, and she had the hopeless eyes of someone who'd seen her dreams fade steadily away.

In the background a man sitting on a day bed motioned for Madison to come in. "Ah, hello, then." His accent was pure English upper class. "Where are you in your day, sport? Tea or bourbon?"

"Bourbon," Madison answered, and looked around

the small apartment. There was a basin and toilet in the corner with a plastic curtain hanging over it for privacy. In the opposite corner sat an oven and another sink with dishes. A tea pot boiled on the stove.

Huxley was thin and slightly stooped the way very tall people sometimes are after a lifetime of bending to carry on conversations. He brought her bourbon in a short glass and smiled. "Heard you've had a spot of trouble, then. Didn't they think to give you any escape passports?"

"Actually, yes," Madison answered. "But the Sendero was looking for a Brit, and since we don't know how they got that information, we thought it wise to start anew."

"Ah, yes," he laughed. "Start anew. Isn't that the way? Cheri, dear, come here, would you? See what we can do for our friend." Then looking back at Madison, he asked, "That eye color real, is it?"

"No. Natural color's green."

"Then let's go with the green, shall we? Cheri, come here, blast you, we've work to do."

Cheri was sitting on the bed in a yoga position, rocking back and forth like a child. She had a doll in her hands. It was made of dark cloth, wearing a handmade dress of bright Andean colors.

Huxley smiled at Madison. "She's mad, that one. Totally barking mad, I tell you. But good once you get her going. No doubt about that. Problem is, she doesn't always want to get going for me anymore. I'm a bore, I think."

Madison went to her and knelt down next to the bed. "I need your help. I'll hold the doll if you'd like," she said gently. Cheri looked at her seriously, then smiled lightly and ran a hand through Madison's hair, testing it the way any stylist would. Madison smiled. "You can do whatever you'd like, you know. I'll leave it entirely to you."

"Barking," Huxley muttered, and disappeared into the one door off the main room. "Got your credit cards worked up this morning," he said, sticking his head through the door. "Once Cheri gets you done right we'll fix the passport. Should have you out of here in a couple of hours."

Madison returned to the Gran Hotel Bolivar and checked in for the second time. This time she used her new name and her new credit cards and her new passport. She had had to make a few stops on the way back to the hotel. She bought a simple, inexpensive room monitoring system, the type used by new mothers to monitor sounds in a nursery, and a set of luggage. Arriving without baggage would have raised questions. She carried the same briefcase, but Huxley had been kind enough to pry away the initialed gold panel while Cheri worked on her hair. By chance she got the same desk clerk, but check-in went as smoothly as it had the first time.

Madison's hair was very short now and dark, almost black. Her eyes were back to their natural green. She wore boots and faded jeans with a jacket that matched, and she spoke to the clerk in Spanish. No one would have recognized her at a glance. Not that it was even a concern. Madison had learned something about disguises in her years with the Company, and the disguises she had used had taught her something about people. A person reacts naturally to whatever is presented to them and they rarely look deeper. Any ordinary, non-threatening persona is accepted at face value. The average person is too absorbed in his or her own world to question another's.

She requested the suite adjacent to the one she had used as Hilary Anne Pitt. Now more waiting.

CHAPTER TEN

Paulina Holgodo and Marta Guzman had been assigned as lookouts each night at target Phoenix. During the day they dropped back several hundred meters and slept while two others watched the objective. Tonight once again Guzman and Holgodo were up front, machine gunner Robby Rodriguez had his M-16 set up just to the right of point, and the balance of the squad was spread out around the airstrip. During their time at Phoenix, they had watched quietly while a total of five small airplanes were loaded and flown away. They had reported the tail number of each aircraft and the direction in which the planes flew. They didn't know how "Singer" passed the Intelligence they collected, didn't know who his commanders might be. But they knew their orders were coming from high up, and the thought that the planes may be intercepted, that the product would never reach the U.S., was what made the hours of intense heat and boredom bearable for them all.

Marta Guzman set up the small satellite dish and dialed in the predetermined frequency. "Singer, this is Fox. Over."

"Go ahead, Fox. Over."

"Got another bird ready to fly at Phoenix, sir," Guzman said, and reported the tail number. "A two-passenger. Over."

"Good work, Fox," answered Harry Carson from the Lima listening post. "After takeoff, neutralize the guards and rig the supply shack to blow. Then move out. We don't want you in one place too long. Next target is called Vegas on your maps. Over."

"Understood, Singer. Copy the Vegas. We're going to need resupply. Rations are running low and it wouldn't hurt to top off our ammo. Over."

"Copy that, Fox. Can you make it to Vegas? Over."

Paulina opened one of the satellite charts and held it for Guzman to see. Vegas was another three miles through very dense jungle. "Yes, sir," Marta Guzman answered. "We can get to Vegas, but we'll have to resupply from there if we're staying in-country. Over."

"Okay, Fox. I'll make arrangements for resupply. Singer out."

Guzman looked at Holgodo. "I guess we're staying a while, huh?"

"Guess so," Paulina said with a nod. "Wish I had a cheeseburger and a nice cool shower." She grabbed her radio and updated Captain Vazquez on the situation.

"Okay," the Captain answered. "Let's get to the rally point and work out a plan of attack."

The rally point in actuality was nothing more than a rubber tree near the banks of a channel four hundred meters from the airstrip. The plan of attack would not be difficult. Only two men guarded the airstrip now. More came when a flight was expected, but they always left afterward.

Paulina knew the assignment would be given to her. She was scout. Her night and jungle skills far exceeded those of the others, and she had been trained on the silenced submachine gun. No one wanted to make too much noise this close to the river. Sound carries over water, and their satellite maps showed a sizeable village not far away. She would circle the strip and go in from the west side, careful to stay out of the way of the M-16 Rodriguez would fire in case she ran into trouble. Friendly fire was just as deadly as enemy fire. The rest of the squad would take up a position well back but within visual range for support.

Vazquez looked at Paulina. "You up for it?"

She nodded. "No problem, sir."

It took her over forty-five minutes to get into position. She had moved slowly, cautiously, not wanting to alert the enemy and lose the element of surprise. Now she was only fifteen meters from her target and she had a clear view of both guards.

They were sitting at a table outside the shack playing cards and smoking. The sweet, musty smell hanging in the air told her immediately that they were not smoking tobacco. That, she thought as she set the selector switch on her rifle to short burst and took aim with the dispassionate ease of a trained soldier, would make her job easier.

To her ears, the silenced crack of the submachine gun sounded incredibly loud, but she knew that from where the guards were sitting, it was barely distinguishable. The evidence of that was the surprise in the other man's face as his partner tumbled out of his chair and hit the ground. And just as Paulina's finger tightened on the trigger a second time, the remaining guard turned and looked directly at her, as if one is awarded a special kind of clairvoyance at the moment before death. Shaken, Paulina let off a quick burst.

"Target neutralized," she reported to her radio.

Captain Vazquez was there in a couple of minutes. He had come alone, leaving the rest of the squad in position. He looked at the bodies. "Good work." Paulina said nothing, hadn't moved since he arrived. "You okay, Holgodo?"

Paulina could see the man in her mind, see the resignation on his face as he looked into the eyes of his killer. She heard Captain Vazquez repeat his question, but the answer seemed to lodge in her throat.

"Shake it off," Vazquez said firmly, slapping a hand against her shoulder. "You did what you were sent to do. Help me get these guys in the shack." He bent down and grabbed one set of ankles.

But Paulina Holgodo didn't budge. "I wonder why

this was so important, Captain," she managed finally. "I mean, they were just men. You know? Just two guys getting stoned and playing cards. They were laughing a couple minutes ago, Captain."

Vazquez faced his young scout. "Let me tell you a secret, Holgodo. When you stomp around in-country with dirt up to your ass and your stomach growling, after awhile you develop a sort of kinship with the enemy. You know? They're the only other people out here and suddenly your differences are blurred. You begin to question. It's reassuring in a way, I guess. It reminds us that we're human, that we're not machines. I bet there's never been a soldier who didn't wonder why they were doing what they were doing. But remember this. It's survival now. If we follow orders, you and me and the rest of the squad just might get out of here alive. It's too late to question our command. You understand?"

"Yes, sir."

"Let's get busy."

It came first as a quiet tapping from the speaker, and Madison McGuire quickly turned her attention to the room monitoring system. She had placed the transmitter in the suite across the hall, the suite she had originally occupied as Hilary Anne Pitt, and the knocking came loud and clear through the receiver in her room. She went to the door and peered through the peephole. A small man in jeans and a dark jacket tapped again at the door across the hall, then pulled something from his pocket. He checked the corridor then squatted down and begin fiddling with the lock. Whatever his business, Madison thought, it was obviously not lock picking. His little hands trembled and it took him a full three minutes to get the door open. When he stepped inside and turned to make a last check of the hall, Madison got her first good look at him before he shut the door. He was light-skinned with round elfin eyes and a face that narrowed to a point at the chin.

She went to her briefcase and assembled the Fiber Viewer, then stepped into the corridor and slid the fiber optic tube under the door. When she switched on the hand-held viewer, she saw him searching the room, opening drawers, impatiently digging through suitcases, shaking trade journals and magazines to see what fell out. And when it looked as if he had found nothing else of interest, he helped himself to the coins she had left on the dressing table.

Madison returned to her room and waited until he pressed the button for the lift, then took the stairs to the lobby. The little man left the hotel immediately, which put an end to her first theory — that of him being a common thief in cahoots with the hotel management, rifling through rooms when the occupants were known to be absent.

She followed him for two blocks before he paused at a street corner and lit a cigarette, idly kicking at a bit of chipped concrete on the sidewalk with one small black shoe. Lima was alive today, as it had seemed to be throughout Madison's stay, with traffic and honking horns and people with too much time on their hands. The ideal situation for a field agent on surveillance.

After a few moments, the rendezvous was

underway. Another man had approached and they seemed to be engaged in a serious conversation. The elf's spidery little hands moved rapidly while he talked. Madison walked a few feet past them and turned back to get a look at the other man's face. She recognized it at once and approached knowing that she risked exposing her cover to the elf, on whom she had no background. But contact was vital.

Their conversation stopped abruptly. The elf smiled and nodded politely. Jose Muro looked at her curiously. "Surely you remember me, Señor Muro," she said in Spanish. "Your friend here just searched my hotel." The smiled dropped off the elf's face and he took a few steps back.

"I did not recognize you," Muro answered. "You look very different."

"So do you," Madison answered, remembering the sleepy, shirtless man who had opened his door to her in Huancayo. "Have you come to Lima to introduce me to your brother-in-law?"

Muro dismissed his elfin friend with a pat on the back and a few quiet words, then faced Madison. "Let me be frank," he said in the voice of a man who was very tired. "Until I know what you want and why you are here, you will not meet Enrique Navarro."

"Let's walk, shall we?"

They headed down the block towards the bustle of the business district, walking slowly, Jose looking at his feet as they went.

"You see," she began carefully. "I represent a private concern who has an ... interest in seeing that Enrique's talents are applied practically. This person believes that your brother-in-law is good for

Peru, that Peru is ready for change. We're prepared to offer assistance wherever Enrique feels it may be needed."

"And why did this private concern of yours not approach us directly?" Jose Muro asked, without looking up from his feet.

Carefully now, Madison thought. "All I can tell you is that there is no hidden agenda. We ask nothing in return for our support. Enrique Navarro's agenda is our agenda and we're offering him the resources to get his movement on its feet — money, technical support, printing presses to get the word out, whatever's needed."

Jose Muro stopped and looked at Madison. "And you, Señorita, what do you get from this?"

Madison smiled. "I get paid. I'm a representative. Nothing more."

Muro reached into his pants pocket and pulled out a wrinkled piece of paper. He unfolded it slowly and showed the picture to Madison. "A representative the Sendero would very much like to find." It was an artist's rendering of Madison's face. "You were wise to change your appearance."

"When can I meet Enrique?"

He folded the sketch back into his pocket. "The Sendero says you are an American Intelligence agent."

"The Sendero has said many things, Jose."

He looked at her for a moment. "I'll let you know."

Madison nodded and gave him her new suite number. "Next time a telephone call will do."

She let him get a block ahead of her before she pulled the earplug from her shirt collar and stuck it in her ear. "Frenchy, old man, did you catch all that?"

"Got it, Scorpion," Greg Abbott answered from the listening post. "Well done. Time for you to see the printers."

The building was a tired bit of white stone cemented into a square block with a long front window of small, dirty panes. It was located just outside Lima's central business district in an area generally avoided by persons of funds. This coupled with a battered economy and frequent power outages might have meant financial failure for another establishment. But this particular printing shop served certain other purposes and therefore it was not profit that kept its doors open.

Madison peered through the small panes and saw that the front counter was unattended, then stepped through the door sideways to prevent the bell from ringing. The shop smelled of ink and rubbing alcohol, and had the untidy look of a place that had not been loved for some time. Uneven stacks of printed flyers with invoices rubber-banded to the tops were piled on the glass counter, presumably waiting to be picked up by customers. Inside the counter a variety of rubber stamps and letter heads and envelopes were displayed, but one had to look to find them under the mess. In the back corner a stack of empty cardboard boxes climbed up the wall.

The door opened behind the counter and a woman stepped through wearing an ink-stained printer's apron. A blue baseball cap sat squarely on her head and a few inches of brown hair stuck out through the band in the back. She seemed to be one of those rare people that age leaves unmarked. Madison put her somewhere between twenty-five and forty. It was impossible to tell where.

The woman smiled and began straightening the counter top. "We have been very busy ..." Her words trailed off and she pushed a bit of dark hair back under the side of her cap. "May I help you?"

Madison had the uncomfortable feeling of having dropped in on a friend and finding the house a mess. "I'm looking for Juan," she said, beginning the prearranged code. "I'm from the travel agency."

"Do you have the tickets?"

"Five of them," Madison answered, completing the code sequence.

"They didn't tell me when you were coming, but I have expected you. I am Carmen."

Madison extended her hand. "McGuire, Madison McGuire."

"Please, come in back where we can talk." She opened the door and led Madison to the back of the shop. It was empty.

They sat down at a small desk. "You run it alone?" Madison asked absently, looking around. "I'd think you'd need some help when the presses are up and running."

She smiled. "I have a big family. They help me in the evenings when I need it. Family you can trust completely. I don't hire outsiders." She took a pen and a note pad from the desk. "Now, what about these flyers? What's the objective?"

No nonsense, Madison thought. Gets straight to it. "We need a sort of profile, really. You know, position on the issues. A little background information. The usual thing. We'll need several thousand."

"Who are we selling this week?" she asked with a laugh.

"A farmer who wants to be a hero, I think," Madison answered with a smile. "The name's Navarro."

The woman stopped writing. "Enrique Navarro?"

"Yes. You've heard of him?"

"The Sendero has offered a reward for him."

"*What*?"

"The founder of the Sendero Luminoso was arrested this morning in a nice middle-class neighborhood here in Lima. I hear he has become very fat in his years of hiding."

Madison was becoming impatient. "You're saying Navarro had something to do with this?"

"A message was received at the Presidential Palace in Lima this morning. Signed by Enrique Navarro. It said that Navarro's Liberation Front would prefer opening a dialogue with the government rather than being forced into taking violent measures. As a gesture of good faith, Navarro used his own Intelligence to discover where the Sendero leader was hiding and gave them the address. So, you see, your farmer is already a hero to some."

"Yes," Madison answered, stunned.

Navarro had gained the trust of Peru's President and dealt the Sendero a devastating blow, but he had also put himself and the operation in danger. The stakes were suddenly considerably higher.

"What else did the letter say?"

Carmen tossed a newspaper at Madison. "Read it

sometime. It can be a very good source for Intelligence." She laughed at her own joke.

Fifteen field agents in Lima alone, and I have to read about it in the bloody paper. She felt her blood pressure rising and glanced up to see Carmen still smiling at her knowingly.

"What?" Madison demanded, but Carmen, guessing that Madison's sense of humor was not at its peak, wisely decided to say nothing and went about silently sketching out the flyer.

CHAPTER ELEVEN

Associated Press. *Lima, Peru — In forty-eight hours a string of car bombings has killed 53 people. Hundreds have been reported injured in separate incidents. The Sendero Luminoso, more commonly known as the Shining Path, Peru's deadly guerrilla group, has launched its most violent offensive since the rebellion began in 1980. The surge of violence is in direct response to the arrest of its feared leader on Thursday.*

Peru's president, Alberto Fujimori, promises to defeat the Sendero Luminoso by the end of his five-year term. But the Shining Path is still five- to eight-thousand strong with capable leadership in place. "In two years we will have control over every major city in Peru including Lima," boasted a member of the Shining Path central committee in a telephone call to a Lima television station ...

"It's going just as we'd expected, Mr. President," said Chief of Staff Robert Little, standing at the Oval Office window peering out onto the lawn. The President sat at his desk, feet up on a corner, ankles crossed. "The Shining Path is sending an enormous amount of muscle towards the cities. Huancayo, Lima, Ayacucho. They're busy trying to deal with both Navarro's Liberation Front and the arrest of their leader. In the meantime our troops have been resupplied and hit two more processing sites without interference."

"When will it be enough?" President Brown asked.

Robert Little turned from the window. "I don't understand."

The President turned in his chair and looked at his Chief of Staff. "How long before we see a measurable drop in the flow of drugs?"

"No one can say that for sure," Little answered uncomfortably. "But I think we'll be able to make an announcement soon. We're hurting them. There's no doubt about it."

"You told me we'd go in, we'd get out fast and we'd get results immediately. I put young lives on the line. I've possibly put my own presidency on the line based on *your* assurances. I'm counting on them to be correct."

With that warning, the Chief of Staff turned back to the window, one eye twitching rapidly. *Sonofabitch, I shouldn't let him see this morning's polls.*

They had arrived separately. Two by helicopter, one had been driven up the pitted dirt hill in a four-wheel drive to Julio Bermudez's sprawling hacienda. The production committee, as they called themselves, never traveled anywhere together. In fact they were rarely found within the same square mile of one another. Security was a major concern for all members of the Cartel. But tonight, for the second time since the Andean Initiative had started, they felt it necessary to bend their own rules and meet in a place where they could talk freely without the worry of U.S. Signal Intelligence invading unsecured telephone lines.

"We've got to do something now, Julio," pleaded Pablo Fernandez, the oldest member of the Cartel's production committee. He was a large man with a fat belly, a full head of silvering hair and bushy eyebrows. The group was gathered casually in Bermudez's living room, sipping cold drinks and nibbling from a tray of appetizers Bermudez's staff had carefully prepared. Fernandez popped a piece of cheese into his mouth. "It's not just a matter of losing a few processing sites anymore. We've lost five planes. Just disappeared. Probably booby-trapped by the soldiers or shot down on their way to the United

States. And it's becoming impossible to find people to work the sites. The rumors have spread throughout the jungle now. People are becoming very frightened, and this is seriously hampering our production ability."

Julio Bermudez sank back into his favorite chair and crossed his legs. "It is under control, Pablo. We must give the American President enough rope and watch him hang himself. The soldiers are a temporary nuisance. That is all. I have a plan to deal with them but it must wait awhile longer."

"We are all reasonable men, Julio," said one of the other members. "Perhaps if you shared your plans with us."

"Of course," Bermudez nodded. "Through contacts in Peru, I have anonymously invited a photographer and a reporter from a popular North American magazine to tour part of the Upper Huallaga Valley. They will first visit the coca growing regions, then be taken into the jungle where they will see for themselves what the American troops have done. Photographs alone can be dismissed. But photographs taken by an American photographer accompanied by an article written by a well-known journalist will carry enough credibility to sufficiently embarrass Señor Brown and his administration, I think. At the same time I have given the Sendero a great deal of money to offer as a reward for the man named Enrique Navarro who is leading a resistance movement against the Sendero. I —"

"*Embarrass. Rewards.*" Pablo Fernandez spat angrily. "This does not solve our problems. I say we send in our own men and kill the American troops. Then our problem will be solved."

There was general approval from the others for this idea, and Bermudez, sensing a revolt, went about regaining control of the meeting. "Are you all so shortsighted?" he roared, standing and shaking his head in disgust. "Don't you see that if we don't do something about this President Brown getting re-elected we are facing four more years of the same? Don't you see that if we do not do something about this new resistance movement, it will threaten the Sendero who protect our processing sites? The United States is behind this movement. I promise you that. They have placed one of their top agents in Lima to ignite the flame and draw the Sendero's attention away from the coca regions."

"And who is the spy in question?" Pablo Fernandez asked.

Bermudez returned to his seat. "I have used my connections to obtain this information," he announced proudly. "Her name is Madison McGuire."

"A woman?" one of the members asked contemptuously.

"A clever and dangerous woman," Bermudez answered. "Who has already escaped capture once and killed two Sendero soldiers. She has no doubt changed her appearance by now. But we will find her, as we will find Enrique Navarro. And the resistance will die with them. We have an informant close to Navarro now. So you see, my friends, we must be patient. We must deal with the long-term problems facing our organization. When we act, it must be action that will solve the problem entirely. When the time is right, we will reclaim the jungle."

"And if we find we cannot deal with the long-term problems?" asked Fernandez ominously.

"Then we will send troops into the jungle and make it safe for our workers again. All I am asking is that you be patient for another week. In that time if you still disagree, if my plan has not won your approval, you have my word that I will do whatever you wish."

It was Jose Muro who had called Madison's suite, but it was his elfin friend with the shaky hands who waited outside for her in the driver's seat of a taxi cab. He smiled pleasantly when she climbed in and then he roared away from the curb.

Since the arrest of the guerrilla leader and the terrorist violence that had followed, Lima had the distinct look of an occupied city. The tense presence of the military could be seen or felt almost anywhere in the city. Armed soldiers in olive green fatigues loitered at major intersections. Army trucks raced the streets, adding more, it seemed, to the chaos of an already unmanageable traffic problem than to the security of the populace.

The elf turned into an alley and explained apologetically that he would have to search her before they could go further. Madison had expected as much, knew she would never be permitted to see Navarro if she were armed, and so she had left her weapon tucked inside the briefcase in the hotel. From somewhere beyond the alley, Madison heard an explosion, felt the hollow rumble of another bomb detonating. As she climbed out of the taxi and submitted to a jittery but thorough search by the elf, she heard shouts on the street and saw a crowd heading in the direction of the explosion. Lima felt more like Beirut every day.

The taxi did not stop again until it reached one of the new shanty-towns on the desert fringes of the city — a community without water or electricity, a community built of cardboard and sand, a community without a blade of grass or a tree or a school for the hundreds of children that called it home. It climbed for acres up the barren stone hillside.

"Walk straight that way," the elf told her, pointing one of his bony little fingers towards a pile of rock. "He will find you."

She started up the hill, looking back once to see that the elf had climbed onto the hood of the taxi and was lighting a cigarette. She was about to light one for herself when she saw a man squatting next to an oil drum on the hillside, talking to a child who had climbed inside. His face was dark and lean; heavy brow ridges shadowed a steady gaze. Her first thought was that his photograph had somehow failed to convey his strength. He stood waiting, watching, neither smiling nor scowling.

"Thank you for seeing me, Señor Navarro," she said, holding out a hand to him.

He seemed to smile without ever adjusting his mouth. It was something that happened in and around the deep set eyes — a softening, a gathering of dark skin at the corners. "I have a feeling that you would have hunted me down if I refused. By the way, Señorita Pitt, your Spanish is excellent."

"It's Hilary," Madison said. "Thank you."

He started walking. "I once knew someone with that name."

He was quiet for a while and Madison thought of

Greg Abbott, of Abbott's unwavering belief that the name would somehow bridge a gap between her and the resistance leader.

Navarro walked slowly, kicking away stones with his worn boots. When he spoke again it was in perfect English. "An interesting message you left for me in Huancayo. About my friend Fritz, I mean. Fritz died two years ago. American Intelligence should have told you that."

Madison felt the swell of anxiety in her chest but she pressed on, deciding it was better not to acknowledge his comment at all. "May I show you something?" she asked, and unfolded a yellow piece of paper from her back pocket. It was one of the flyers Carmen had worked up at the printing shop. It listed his views on everything from coca eradication to the Sendero Luminoso. It quoted portions of his letter to Peru's President where he demanded the government implement the programs it had been promising — irrigation projects to open new areas for farming, protection for farmers from Sendero attacks.

Madison watched him read it over several times. He stopped occasionally and stood with the flyer held at his side, thinking it over. He was silent for some time, and his face, to Madison, was unreadable. Navarro's pauses were like none she had ever known. They kept you waiting on pins and needles.

"How did you choose the name?" he asked finally.

"Pardon me?"

His voice never lost its calm. It was deep and fluid and she felt his dark eyes locking on her. "The name," he repeated. "Hilary. Did you choose it because it was my wife's name?" He held up one finger. "Before you answer, I must tell you that I left Huancayo soon after your visit, and I saw the remnants of the Sendero roadblock. Only someone trained in anti-terrorist tactics could have done so much damage and walked away. So please, do not insult my intelligence further by lying."

"My cover was established before we knew about your wife," Madison answered. "I'm sorry."

"I see," he said quietly. "And now, please tell me who you are and why you have come here."

"My name is Madison McGuire. I've been sent here to offer you assistance in furthering your agenda."

"It is *your* agenda that I'm interested in."

Madison stopped and faced him. "You and I, Enrique — our countries, our lives — like it or not, are inescapably linked. We both stand to lose if the Sendero campaign is successful. It's just a matter of wanting the same thing for different reasons. We're offering you the resources you need to turn your Liberation Front into a significant force. And we're offering without asking anything in return."

They walked down a crowded row of makeshift huts. A group of women waited their turn in line to wash clothes in a metal tub. Water is precious in the barraidas, Enrique told her. An old man leaned against a half wall of cement blocks, playing a wood flute. A group of children at his feet sang quietly, solemnly.

"Hear that?" Enrique asked. "That is the sound of hope. We are a hopeful people. There is music and dancing here every night." He stopped and smiled. "When the guerrillas first began their attacks on the power stations, Lima was blacked out completely. I was in Lima that night. People came out of their homes and businesses and lined the streets. And do you know why?" He walked again. "They wanted to see the stars without the city lights blocking their view. That is what I love about Peru."

"I'm sorry," Madison said quietly and her answer, or the earnestness of it, had surprised him. He looked at her curiously. "You love Peru, I know," she continued. "I'm sorry for what's happening here now."

They were quiet for a while, Madison studying the rubble around her, fighting away the flies and the smell. As they walked, Enrique nodded to familiar faces, stopping sometimes to speak for a moment. They all seemed to know him. A line of children had formed behind them. Madison heard a giggle and turned to look. They scattered, laughing.

"The guerrillas will return to Huancayo one day soon," he said. "The government soldiers will not stay in the small cities for long. The Army is already spread too thin. The Sendero will come with submachine guns and machetes and bombs, and force the peasants to help in their attacks. They will take Huancayo and then they will come for Lima."

"Yes," Madison agreed. "Unless they meet resistance."

He stopped in front of a small tent, reached inside for a blanket and spread it on the ground. He lowered himself easily into a yoga position and nodded for Madison to join him. "And I suppose that I am to be that resistance since American soldiers cannot come here uninvited. You want me to do the fighting for you. Is that it?"

Madison found two cigarettes in her jacket

pocket, offered one to the resistance leader and took one for herself. "Seems an odd question," she said calmly. "Let's review the facts, shall we? It was *you* who turned the Sendero leader over to the government. You, Señor Navarro, put a price on your own head. And it was you and you alone who convinced a handful of workers and farmers that they could stand up against the guerrilla threat." She paused and lit both their cigarettes. She watched him for a moment. "They'll have to do just that one day, you know. Civilians going head-to-head with trained guerrillas. I'd think you'd feel an obligation to even the odds a bit."

"I was angry," he said so quietly that he might have been confessing. "My sister was killed, my country is dying. Do you know what it's like to watch your country die a little each day?"

"Yes," Madison answered, looking directly into his eyes.

A sad smile crossed his face. "I wanted to fight. I don't know. I wanted them to pay somehow for what they've done. But I am no leader. I cannot bear the responsibility for so many lives."

Madison looked up and down the rows of huts and boxes and oil drums. She looked at the children playing, at the men loitering, at the women washing and cooking. "Where do these people come from, Enrique? Why are they here?"

"The mountains, the interior, their ancestral home," he answered. "They cannot live there any longer, they cannot support themselves. They've been driven into the city by the people who claim to be fighting in their name. The Sendero steals from them, slaughters them, humiliates them. And the

143

government," he added with a bitter laugh, "it makes promises it never intends to keep. You wonder who they are. They are just people like you and me and they dream of going home one day."

"An improbable dream," Madison said. "Too bad."

"No," Navarro snapped. "It *is* possible. The government will one day be pressured into controlling the guerrillas, into providing irrigation for the farmers, into building schools and educating our children. Let these people keep their dreams. It is possible. I know it."

"Spoken like a true leader," Madison said.

He sat quietly for a few moments, then turned to her. "I am out of my depth."

"We all are. But it's too late to turn back."

CHAPTER TWELVE

The taxi cab was sitting at the bottom of the hill, and the elf lingered on the bonnet, picking at a bit of flaking orange paint and smoking what Madison reckoned must have been his tenth cigarette since she left him there an hour ago. He sprang to his feet and jerked open the rear door. She asked to be returned to her hotel.

Five minutes into the drive, the little man made one congenial attempt at small talk, but Madison barely heard a word he said and her clipped one-word answers cut him short before he got up to speed.

She wondered what would happen now, to Navarro, to Peru. There were still a few more steps on her end — getting Navarro settled into a safe house and keeping him there until they hauled in a flock of babysitters for him, advising Greg Abbott to have the flyers distributed that would help gather popular support in the outlying areas. But, technically her part of the assignment could be labeled a success. She had found Navarro, convinced him of his importance, made the agreement she had been sent to make. Now the details would be worked out by the head office, by analysts and controllers. They would send weapons and trainers and turn Navarro's farmers into soldiers. They would send strategists in business suits from Langley to make them charts and teach them how a real war is run. They would send professional soldiers in plain clothes from God only knew where, and put them on the front lines to give the Sendero a surprise when they marched on Huancayo again. And, whatever else happened, Peru would be forever changed. She sighed and tried to shake the uneasy feeling of having just handed the young leader a live grenade.

It is this kind of questioning that every field agent knows intimately, a kind of self-interrogation that comes with the tension of the field. A kind of awareness that sweeps into the consciousness, and, for an agent — so say Langley's experts — it can be fatal. She had the urgent sensation — just briefly but hazardous for any length of time — of knowing

Peru, of loving it, of wanting to stop the wheels from turning, and to let Peru heal itself.

The taxi nosed its way slowly up the block towards the hotel. Madison turned away from the window, away from her thoughts, and noticed the elf's eyes on her in the rearview mirror.

It was pure instinct that caused her sudden alarm, caused her to yell for him to stop a hundred yards away from the front entrance. Startled, he hit the brakes, but one wiry little hand quickly reached for the lights and pulled them on twice. Madison jerked her door handle up and saw the elf dive down into the front seat as she tumbled out the back door and squatted near the taxi, eyes and ears pounding with fear and rage, her mind trying desperately to formulate some plan in the face of the elf's betrayal.

As if choreographed, two vehicles swung around in front of the hotel, tires squealing in unison, racing towards them, men with submachine guns leaning out the passenger windows. She had to move. But there was nowhere to go. No cover.

Do it! Hurry. She opened the front door and yanked the little man by his collar, sliding him across the seat on his belly and out onto the concrete.

. . . Then the burst of automatic weapons. Bullets exploded into the windshield and ripped through the top of the vinyl seats as the killers made their first pass. Seconds later, she heard the engines gunning again, heard the tires squeal, knew they were coming back.

Quickly. She dove into the front seat, slammed the taxi into gear and jammed the accelerator into the floorboard. A cloud of black exhaust rolled from the tail pipe and deteriorated into the white Peruvian sky. The taxi hesitated, then coughed again and lurched sluggishly from the curb like a tired fighter after five rounds. In one flash, Madison realized that she had just made herself skipper of a sinking ship.

Christ. Where am I? The Plaza, she remembered, the Plaza San Martin was just on the other side of the hotel. Vendors, people, the pavement cafe. *Cover.*

The two vehicles were coming back fast in the rearview mirror, gunmen leaning out the windows ready for their second swipe at her.

... Fire again, pinging off the cab, fracturing the back window. *Shit.*

At the hotel entrance, she let the old cab veer off without her and flung herself through the passenger door. She scarcely noticed that her jeans had ripped at the knees or that blood trickled down her shins when she got to her feet and made a dash for the entrance — a moving target, running, head down, zig-zagging as the bullets gnawed at the pavement around her and shattered one of the glass doors.

She had nearly made it through the entrance when she caught the horrified expression of ' the porter as she charged by him and a round of bullets tore into his chest.

At the back end of the hotel, the Square was bustling with activity. No one seemed to have been alarmed by what they all must have heard. But then in Lima, the unthinkable had become daily fare.

Violence, it seemed, was always lurking around the corner like a patient mugger ready to spring.

She slowed her pace as much as she could, considering her heart was going great guns, and walked past the pavement cafe towards the street vendors lined up along the wall of the bank building. But her feather duster and plastic ruler man was nowhere to be seen. Probably reassigned, she thought bitterly, and added that to the list of Intelligence Langley had forgotten to share with her.

Suddenly, a hand on her shoulder. "I've been waiting for you." The voice was male, familiar. Madison spun around to see Anthony the guide smiling at her. "I almost did not recognize you. I think you should ask your hairdresser for your money back." He laughed loudly.

"Where's the Toyota?"

It might have been the torn jeans or the bloodied shins that alerted him once he took a moment to look her over, but most probably it was the dead calm in her voice, the crazed look in her green eyes and the fingers that clasped tightly around his wrist. Whatever had triggered his alarm, Anthony sensed danger and took a step back. "I see that I have come at a bad time."

"Oh, no," Madison said, tightening her grasp. "You've come at precisely the right time. Now, wrap your arm round my shoulder and let's walk to your truck. Just out for a nice stroll. Right? No hurry. No, no, don't look around." She wrapped an arm around his waist and snuggled her head into his shoulder.

"What's happening?" he whispered.

"You don't want to know."

"Are we going to be killed?"

"I hope not. Do you have a gun?"

"Yes, in the truck, but ... where are we going?"

"I'll tell you later," Madison answered, wondering if the elf's betrayal had reached Navarro yet, hoping they would get to the young leader in time.

Evening came quietly to Lima, an evening entirely without movement of air or cloud, without wind or rain. And even though there were no visible clouds, Madison could not find a star in the sky. Nearby a mighty ocean was this minute gearing itself up for its winter attack on miles of desert sand coast. Nearby too, guerrillas planned their next attack, activists designed their revolution, pavement artists shadowed their prey, sinking into Lima's shadows. But here, looking up the hill at the shanty-town, Madison found no reminders that there was a world apart from this at all. No smell of salt air, no desert heat, no protests or car bombs, no evidence that the Sendero might be closing in any minute, no sounds to suggest that they were here already. Just the quiet torches from another barriada burning over the city.

"Quiet tonight," Anthony whispered anxiously as they stood looking at the hilltop community where Madison had first met Enrique Navarro. "It is still early. Yet I hear no children."

"Yes," Madison agreed, remembering something Enrique had said. *There is music and dancing here every night.*

"I'm coming with you."

Madison shook her head. "Wait here. Keep the engine running. Should be a short visit."

"No. I'm coming," he repeated, this time with a bit more force.

Madison took a breath and gathered her patience. "Something's wrong up there, Anthony. We both agree on that, don't we? Now, *I have* to go up there. *You,* on the other hand, can stay here. Danger up there. Safety down here. What do you think would be the smartest thing for you to do?"

Anthony started walking. "I am not a dull child," he said angrily. "No matter what you think. I am a man and I'm going with you."

"Lovely," Madison muttered. "But you're on your own and I'm keeping the gun."

"Just as well. I haven't shot it in years anyway."

Madison ran to catch up. "You've kept it clean though, haven't you? In good condition and all that?"

Anthony shrugged. "I am just a poor dumb guide, Señorita. How would I understand such things?"

"Point taken. I apologize." She touched his arm to slow him down. "A few more yards and we'll be in the light. If the Sendero's here, they'll be watching the hill. Stay in the shadows if you can and stay down."

Then, the muted spit from a silenced weapon sliced the air and dug into the dirt between them. Madison knocked Anthony to the ground and they rolled down the hill, finding cover behind a mound of sand and concrete blocks. Madison's mind was churning. Something wasn't quite right. The Sendero didn't operate this way, didn't let off warning shots.

"Mother of God," Anthony muttered, panting.

"They are here already." Madison started to stand and Anthony yanked her back down. "Are you crazy?"

She yelled to the hilltop. "It's Madison McGuire, Enrique. I've come with a friend. Your man with the taxi betrayed us both. They'll be coming for you next, I'm afraid. Don't have much time."

For several seconds they heard only their own breathing. Then a woman's voice came from the hill, inviting them up, but warning them to approach slowly.

They rose up from behind the sand mound and looked up the hill. "Amazing," Madison said. "Look at that, Anthony. Just look at them. They've had enough."

The line stretched across the hilltop, a human wall of women and men silhouetted by the glow of the torches, guarding what possessions they had left, guarding the man who had restored their hope.

Anthony was watching the ground as he struggled up the hill. He had acquired a slight limp in the last few minutes and Madison thought he might have twisted something in the fall. She brushed at the sand on his jacket. "Almost there, old man. Don't worry. Ah, there he is now. Navarro in the flesh."

The line parted to let them through. Enrique Navarro stood soberly with a 9mm stuffed in his waistband and a steel pipe in his hands. Madison could see his dark eyes flickering in the torch light. "I know what happened," he said, and by his voice Madison knew his friend's betrayal had genuinely hurt him. "I had you followed. I thought it was you who could not be trusted."

"We've got to get you out," Madison said, glancing at her watch.

"They've already been here," Navarro broke in. "Four of them. They did not expect such a welcoming committee, I think." He smiled and waved a hand. "Here are some of the brave people who saved my life tonight."

Madison looked at the group. They were young and old. They carried sticks and bats and bricks. A few held rifles and handguns, but only a very few. "You know they'll be back, don't you? We've got to get you to a safe place."

"And leave my friends to fight alone?" Navarro asked. "No. I cannot."

"You endanger your friends by staying," Madison insisted. "It's you the Sendero wants. These people won't have to fight if you're gone."

"And if you're wrong?" Navarro asked. "If the guerrillas come back, what happens to these people then?"

"Nothing that one man could rectify anyway," Madison answered, and knew immediately that it was not the answer Navarro had wanted.

He looked at her for some time, stared at her without the limitations of finesse or deception, studied her with artless curiosity the way a healthy child might look at a sick one, and Madison realized that the man who had decided to accept her help for his movement did not particularly like her or what she stood for. She wanted to tell him that she was not indifferent to the people here, to their safety, their lives. She wanted to tell him that her job had changed the moment they had made an agreement, that her central concern was now his safety alone,

153

that it was vital to the movement. She wanted to right herself in his eyes, wanted to defend what he perceived as detachment and callousness, wanted to explain that he must be protected at all cost. But even Madison was beginning to lose faith in the doctrine of the greater good. It was a decision he would have to make.

"Do what you have to do," she told him without explanation, without malice or resentment, and started down the hill with Anthony in tow, wondering all the while how she would explain to her controller that the operation was first a success then a dismal failure all in one day. What would Abbott say? What would Langley say when they read her report and discovered that Enrique Navarro had been frightened suddenly away by one objective observation on her part? They would say that her lack of subtlety had cost the operation, that Navarro wasn't yet ready for a dose of reality. Innocence is something that must be taken slowly. Truths must be implied, fact insinuated.

"What happens now?" Anthony asked when they reached the truck.

They heard footsteps. Madison turned and saw Enrique Navarro coming towards them, head down, which was his usual way of walking, watching his old boots sink into the sand hill. She leaned against Anthony's truck and waited.

"You were right, of course," Navarro said. "I only endanger the people with my presence. I am yours now. I accept your offer."

CHAPTER THIRTEEN

The President of the United States stepped onto the White House lawn with the First Lady on his arm. The Chief of Staff and three aides emerged moments later. Marine One waited on the grass to deliver the President to Camp David for a weekend strategy session with his senior campaign advisors.

As the President walked toward the helicopter, he unavoidably neared the reporters and cameras lined up against the roped-off area of the lawn. The First Lady disengaged herself from his arm, gracefully turning the spotlight over to her husband while he smiled and waved.

"Mr. President," shouted a well-known member of the electronic media. "How do you respond to the article this morning in *Newsday*?"

The President kept moving, not wanting to encourage more questions, and shrugged. "Haven't seen the article, Paul. I'll let you know."

Another shout. Louder this time. Impossible to ignore. "Mr. President, *Newsday* published several photographs of dead workers at processing sites in Peru that suggest the United States is currently involved in combat operations there. These people were civilian workers, Mr. President, local natives and peasants. How do you respond, sir, and is this part of your Andean Initiative?"

He glanced at his Chief of Staff as he turned to face the reporters. He had to comment. He dared not leave that question hanging in the dirty air over Washington during an election year. *Damn, how did this get out?*

"First of all let me say that the United States of America has never and will never be involved in any campaign aimed at taking the lives of innocent civilians." He moved yet closer to the rope and looked at the reporters. "To suggest such a thing is not only outrageous, it's irresponsible. And it's a little funny that this should pop up so close to the election."

Another voice. Female. "Are you denying that we have troops in the jungles of Peru, Mr. President? And are you suggesting that the photographs are simply political dirty tricks?"

The President raised his hands in another shrug.

"I can only tell you what I know, and that is that we are not involved in any unauthorized military activity in Peru or anywhere else."

More shouts. More questions. Cameras flashed and video recorders whirred. The President started up the steps of the helicopter. When he reached the top and turned to wave, he felt a drop of perspiration trickle down the back of his neck and into his shirt collar. Knowing that he should have reserved comment, knowing they wanted his first reaction, knowing that they would use it against him later if they could, he had just lied to the Press. It was not his first major political lie. But he knew very well that it might turn out to be his most costly.

He climbed into Marine One and looked at Chief of Staff Robert Little. "Get Mitchell Colby and James Jefferies up to Camp David," he ordered. *"And get a copy of that goddamned article."*

Mitchell Colby walked into the third floor office and pulled the sliding glass door shut behind him. "Straight from the cipher room," Senior Analyst for Operations Warren Moss told him, handing the Director the message.

Colby fished around in his jacket pocket for his glasses, found a chair and snapped the message up to reading level. "Good news," he reported. "McGuire got Navarro. They're in the Lima safe house. Smart man. The Shining Path would have blown his ass off." He returned the gold-rimmed spectacles to his pocket and reached for an inside line to Fred Nolan's office. "Maxim One is ready to go full force," he told his Deputy Director. "I want the department heads in my office in an hour. And get hold of the Secretary, Fred. Be sure that controller he's got down there has the propaganda campaign going."

He replaced the receiver and stood to leave. "Get your crew on this right away, Warren. Might as well get yourself in the loop now. You'll be head of Operations one day."

"Yes, sir," Moss answered excitedly.

Colby had taken a step into the corridor when Moss summoned him back for a call from the White House Chief of Staff. The Director listened quietly for a moment then disconnected the line and rang Fred Nolan back. "Little just found out about the *Newsday* piece." He chuckled. "The President got ambushed on the White House lawn by a bunch of reporters. I've got to go to Camp David. Ready phase two and activate the extra muscle. We need them in place in Huancayo right away. As soon as our planners get to Lima and meet with Navarro they can get started training his farmers. I'll see you tonight."

Strings of contemporary, well-kept suburbs along Lima's Pacific coast contrasted greatly with the Spanish colonial architecture and dingy offices of downtown. On a palm-lined street in one of the wealthier areas, nestled comfortably between the great bluffs that overlooked the Pacific and the working class neighborhood of La Victoria, sat a rambling white brick estate with black lattice work and a fresh coat of red paint on the shutters. To the residents of the area, it was like any other house in the neighborhood. The owners, it was rumored, were connected with the Agency for International Development (AID) and did quite a lot of traveling. What the neighbors did not know was that the house had been used for many purposes over the years and AID was frequently used as cover by the CIA.

Madison punched in the code on the electronic lock, turned off the security system and stepped aside for Enrique Navarro and Anthony to enter. Heavy drapes hung in front of a wide sea window and filtered out nearly all the natural light. Lamps with claret shades that matched the curtains burned on the end tables. The furniture was expensive, soft cream-colored leather. Portraits of nameless men and women hung on the staircase wall that led to the upstairs bedrooms. A portrait of Peru's President in a gallant pose hung over the marble mantel. Madison looked at the ceiling fan and wondered absently if there was a safe house, no matter how grand, anywhere in the world that did not smell of burned coffee and cigarette smoke.

"What now?" Navarro asked, in the agreeable voice of a man who had turned his life over to others.

"Give me your sizes and I'll have some clothes rounded up for you," Madison told him. "Your bedroom is upstairs. Last door on the right. They've promised there'll be food in the kitchen. Make yourself comfortable. Oh, by the way, leave the shades drawn on the upstairs windows and let me know if you need to make any calls."

Madison watched him walk up the stairs and turned to Anthony. "Drink, old man? Think I owe you one, don't I?"

Anthony followed her into the next room where they found a huge color television set and a well-stocked bar. He peeked at the downstairs room and smiled when he saw a billiards table waiting like an invitation. "I almost forgot why I was looking for you at the hotel," he said, pouring a shot of warm whiskey into a glass. "My brother has friends who are Senderistas. They heard there are soldiers in the jungles of Peru where the coca processing is done. And they are not DEA agents or Peruvian police. They are a small group of special American army soldiers sent to destroy processing sites. The Sendero is very unhappy about this. They alone control the coca regions. It could be very dangerous for your soldiers."

The den was dark. Madison rambled over to a window and parted the curtain. Nothing much to see there. A backyard that sloped down into sand. A child's swing-set waiting dully for no one. From upstairs she heard water rushing through the pipes and knew Enrique had found the shower.

She looked back at Anthony. "Has your brother had access to information like this before?"

"Yes," Anthony nodded.

"And it's panned out? Been reliable?"

"Oh, yes," Anthony said proudly. "My brother himself believes in the Sendero. His friends are very involved and very knowledgeable."

"Would you excuse me, Anthony? I have some

160

things to do. Have another drink if you'd like. Pick a bedroom for yourself. I'm afraid I'll have to keep you here for a while. Security and all that."

Anthony sprang to his feet. "I cannot stay. I have a family that will worry."

"Shouldn't be long." Anthony looked at her helplessly as she started out of the room. She smiled. "You'll be fine. Think of it as a vacation."

"You do not have to hold me here. I will tell no one of this place. I swear."

Madison nodded. "I believe you. Really. Just following the rules."

"What's Navarro like?" Greg Abbott asked into the secure telephone.

"Mortal," Madison answered. "Frightened sometimes, brave others." All of which she understood effortlessly. "He's a good man, I think."

"You did a good job," Abbott told her and she knew he was smiling. "Sit tight for a while. The planners will be here in a day or two to take over. In the meantime do what you can to make him comfortable. Brief him. Let him know what to expect."

"He'll need some fresh clothes." She gave him the sizes. "And he'd like the newspaper delivered in the morning, please. Also, I need my things picked up from the hotel. Had a spot of trouble this afternoon. Left everything. Oh, I've brought someone along. He'll need clothes too. Same size. Thought I'd keep him here till we learn a little more about him. Run a check for me, would you? The name is Anthony Castillo."

"Jesus," Abbott muttered.

"I know," Madison answered. "It wasn't planned. He was there at the right time, I'm afraid, and I needed his help. Nice fellow, actually, but let's be sure."

"I'll run the check."

"By the way," Madison said casually, "are we running a jungle op?" She listened closely for his reaction.

Greg Abbott turned to Harry Carson who sat on the opposite side of the listening post, scribbled a note and put the call on the speakers. "You're over your clearance," Abbott told her.

Madison continued. "Word is, there are Americans in the jungle. The Sendero is understandably concerned. Peru would be too, I imagine. It being a sovereign nation and all that. Sticky business. Wouldn't want it on my plate if I were you."

Carson and Abbott looked at each other. "Where did you get this?" Abbott asked.

"Sorry, old boy. Can't give you that. Rule of mine, really. Gets confusing with too many cooks. You understand."

"I don't want a name," Abbott said. "I'm just trying to establish whether or not it comes from an inside source."

"It doesn't," Madison answered. "It came in at street level."

Greg Abbott was quiet for a moment, then answered only, "I'll have the things you ordered delivered by morning." The line went dead.

The setting was rustic, very masculine. The President's desk was an antique — double-sided with black leather-tipped corners. The furniture was reddish brown leather and heavy. The President wore casual slacks and a western shirt and stood gazing at the pine trees through the huge window behind his desk. Even James Jefferies, the Secretary of State, a man known for his formality, had loosened his tie and removed his jacket. Life was easier at Camp David. The public and the media could be held at bay here. Temporarily anyway.

"The FBI has people in New York questioning the journalist and the photographer," Mitchell Colby added. "We're betting the Colombian Cartel arranged the whole business."

"Peru's ambassador has asked for an appointment," said Chief of Staff, Robert Little. His eye had started to twitch and he ran his index finger over the rim to calm it, something Little did often.

"He wants an explanation," James Jefferies added.

The President did not turn from the window. "Put him off until Monday." The Chief of Staff nodded and made a note that no one else could see.

"I think we should get a statement out to the Press right away saying that whatever's happening in Peru it's happening without American involvement," Jefferies said. "A complete denial. Use a low level spokesperson and give the whole thing as little attention as possible."

"We're on that already," Little said. "The statement will be made at the White House this afternoon. Best to keep the President as far away from any of this as possible."

Mitchell Colby cleared his throat and shifted in his chair. "I hope we're all agreed that it's time to extract my people. They can't possibly continue with any success now. The Lima operation is showing a great deal of promise. We can focus on that end."

"I agree," Jefferies said. "The Lima op may not net quick results, but the long term implications are very positive. Let's extract the jungle unit and put everything we've got into Lima."

Robert Little shook his head. "But is there a way to get them out without alerting Peruvian authorities?"

The Director of Central Intelligence glanced at Little then looked at the President. "We got them in without even a blip on a radar screen. We can sure as hell get them out."

"We got them in," the Chief of Staff pointed out, "before any of this came to light. They're watching now and you can bet they're watching close. The government's watching its airspace and the Shining Path's watching the jungle. If we lose a helicopter during the extraction, there'll be no way to cover it." *And the President of the United States looks like a liar.* He didn't say it. He didn't have to.

The President sat down. He had a reserved calm about him that always took the forefront in the midst of a crisis. "Those kids risked their lives for this country," he said quietly. "In good faith. They trust their command, and they trust that what they're doing is right. Whatever the political ramifications, Robert, I know you can't be suggesting that we leave them down there."

"No, no. Of course not. Only that we leave them until this thing blows over. When it's safe, we bring them home."

The President looked at Colby. "Is that a possibility?"

Colby pursed his lips thoughtfully and nodded. "They can go ten days without resupply. Maybe even a little longer without discomfort. After that it gets tough."

They heard the quick footsteps on the hardwood floors before the knock came at the door. It was one of the President's aides with an urgent message for the Director. Colby dismissed the aide with a nod and fumbled for his glasses while all three men watched quietly.

"Peru has secured its airspace," Colby told them gravely. "They're giving us twenty-four hours to give them a satisfactory explanation before they announce the move publicly. My sources inside the Presidential Palace say Peru's prepared a statement saying it is within the rights of a sovereign nation to protect its borders. They're cancelling all joint U.S./Peruvian operations and all U.S. military flights will need special clearance. The message will be sent through diplomatic channels later today."

Colby folded the paper neatly in half and removed his glasses. "I hope it goes well with the Ambassador. If we have to fly into secured airspace to get those kids out, the stakes will be considerably higher."

* * * * *

Paulina Holgodo opened a small unmarked plastic bottle and popped three 200mg Ibuprofen tablets into her mouth. Her head hurt, her shoulders ached and both ankles were swollen with minor sprains. The physical and mental stress was beginning to weigh heavily on the entire squad, and six hundred milligrams every couple of hours barely kept the young scout's mind off her aches and pains.

The team had been on the move for two nights solid without enemy contact. Or was it three nights? Paulina had lost track. They had arrived at several processing sites, targets carefully charted on their satellite maps. They had found a few empty barrels lined with residue from the acid wash used in processing coca leaves, and jute sacks with a few leaves left inside. They had found cigarette butts and footprints and tire tracks. But no processors.

Paulina switched on her goggles and studied one of the trails she had picked up two hours ago. It was at least a day old, maybe two. Nothing was going to happen tonight, she thought with a mixture of relief and aggravation, still unsure whether the combat or the calm was hardest to cope with.

After another hour, she found the prearranged rally point that had been marked on her map, and refilled her canteen from the river while she waited for the rest of the squad to catch up. Leaning against a tree trunk, she closed her eyes, and focused her mind on memory. But home was so far away from the dark of the jungle, she could barely even visualize it now.

"Trails are all cold, sir," she told Vazquez when

the team arrived. "Good news, huh? We've scared them off. Maybe we can go home soon."

"Yeah," Captain Vazquez answered with an encouraging nod, but he knew that his squad was young, knew that for all their talent and training they still lacked the intuition that comes with experience. And Captain Vazquez could not shake the uncomfortable feeling that something wasn't right. But then the quiet had always frightened him.

When he was a small child, his family had lived in a trailer park near Miami. One Saturday afternoon his parents had hauled the children out of the rocking mobile home in the midst of a brutal thunderstorm. They had huddled in a ditch, five of them in all, shaking and drenched, for fifteen minutes until the wind and the rumbling had passed and the quiet returned. Black clouds drifted away like ghosts in a young boy's eyes and the sky cleared to yellow.

They had been back inside their warm home for only a few minutes when the roar came like a jet engine, when the wind ripped the roof off the trailer and brought the walls tumbling in on them.

Captain Vazquez understood how deceptive quiet can be.

CHAPTER FOURTEEN

Chief of Staff Robert Little had returned to the White House early in the afternoon, leaving the President at Camp David where he would be kept at a safe distance from the media. It was time for some damage control, and Robert Little knew very well that the only way to deal with the media was to throw them a sizable bone now and then.

He looked at the reporter who had just been shown into his White House office. The man worked as a Washington correspondent for the *New York*

Post. He was aggressive, up-and-coming, hungry, young. Young enough, Little hoped, to be impressed by the Chief of Staff.

Little stood and shook the man's hand enthusiastically, offered him coffee or tea, let him know it was all right to smoke, and smiled at him over his desk.

"I like your style," Little lied. "That's why I invited you. As long as we have an understanding, we'll get along just fine. You may not use my name or office. I will be quoted only as an official source. Is that clear?"

"Perfectly," answered the reporter, pulling a writing pad from his leather bag. "You tell me what you want the public to believe and I print it. It's called a controlled leak, I believe."

Little clicked his tongue against his front teeth and studied the young man. He was arrogant. Little hated arrogance. "I'm giving you a story. Take it or leave it."

The reporter smiled. "Don't get me wrong. I'll take it. I just thought we should have our cards on the table. What's happening in Peru?"

"To be honest, I can only speculate. But I can tell you for sure that we are not involved."

The reporter looked at him for a moment. "Okay. Then let's speculate."

"Just in the last three weeks," Little said, leaning forward on his elbows, "since we've stepped up our anti-drug campaign, our planes have intercepted five illegal aircraft bound for the U.S. We have confiscated over sixty million dollars in high grade cocaine. The coca was grown and processed in Peru, but the proceeds go to the Colombian Cartel that controls the area and supports the guerrilla movement in Peru."

"So you're saying the Cartel is involved somehow?" the reporter asked, surprised.

Little nodded. "This administration made a promise during the last election that it's never forgotten. We said we would slow the flow of drugs into this country and we have. We've been a constant source of irritation and financial loss for the Colombian drug lords. They're striking back now in a typically predictable and barbaric fashion, slaughtering their own peasant workers and inviting American journalists who should know better to photograph their handiwork."

"You have proof of this?"

Little nodded. "We're working on it."

The reporter looked up from his pad. "How do you feel about what you saw in the photographs?"

"Personally? Off the record?" Little received a nod from the reporter. "I wouldn't give a shit if the earth opened up and swallowed every one of the bastards. If they're processing drugs that will end up in this country, they are not innocent bystanders."

Robert Little watched the reporter leave his office and leaned back in his chair, satisfied that the story would appear in tomorrow's newspapers and kill what was gearing up to be a scandal.

His telephone buzzed. "Intercept from SINGER," the voice announced.

"Send it over," Little answered with a smile. He was feeling quite proud of himself. A few days ago at the National Security Agency, he had thrown a great deal of weight around until he had arranged

170

for the NSA to intercept all communications destined for Langley using the code word SINGER, which was the code used by Harry Carson in the Lima listening post, a code word that signaled communication on the status of the jungle operation. The NSA was to flag all the intercepts for his eyes only and contact him immediately. This way he would know what was happening in Peru without being at the mercy of the Director of Central Intelligence.

The message arrived by uniformed carrier thirty minutes later.

****TOP SECRET****
****SINGER REPORT****
POSSIBLE SECURITY PROBLEMS WITH MAXIM-TWO. OPERATIONAL INFORMATION READILY AVAILABLE AT STREET LEVEL AND PICKED UP BY MAXIM-ONE HEAD OPERATIVE. ADVISE EXTREME CAUTION AND SUGGEST IMMEDIATE EXTRACTION OF ALL PERSONNEL.
****END INTERCEPT****

Robert Little buzzed his assistant. "Get me director Colby at CIA." A few moments later his phone lit up and he lifted the receiver. "Mitch," he said cheerfully. "How's it going? Anything new with Maxim Two?"

"I'm afraid it's not good," Mitchell Colby answered. "Security's shot to hell and back. We've got to get those kids out before the Shining Path does it for us."

Little hadn't expected Colby to be honest. "Give it some time."

Colby sighed. "I'm not sure how much time we've got."

"Tell me something, Mitch. Why didn't you warn the President about the *Newsday* article? You had to know about it."

"The last time I went over your head," the Director answered with a grin in his voice, "you almost wet yourself."

"You crafty old sonofabitch," Little muttered. "By the way, you should talk to your friends at NSA. They're a little slow in delivering your mail. The cable from SINGER came in hours ago."

Madison stepped back into the safe house after saying good-bye to Anthony. The background check had gone well, Greg Abbott reported earlier. But Madison bad never really believed anything else about Anthony. She had released him happily and waved as he drove through the driveway gates. Another face in her career, another good-bye.

Enrique Navarro was sitting in the den, elbows on his knees, hands holding his chin. The television was very loud, but he wasn't watching. His coffee mug was full on the floor beside him. On the coffee table sat an uncapped bottle of imported whiskey. He hadn't shaved.

"Here I am," he said in a slightly mystified voice, as Madison sat beside him. "The man who would save Peru. I ask you, who could face that sober?" He tried to laugh but his heart wasn't in it.

From the kitchen she heard the mounting whine

of a tea kettle she'd put on the stove, but she didn't move. She waited. Even now, half drunk and immersed in self-pity, Enrique Navarro had a way about him that made you wait. She always sensed there might be something extraordinary on the horizon when he spoke.

"The Sendero began like this." His dark eyes found a spot on the carpeting and stayed there. "With an idea. A promise." He turned to her and squeezed one hand into a fist as he spoke. "I am on the verge of something I can barely conceive of, and it petrifies me. What will become of me when I too am powerful, when my Liberation Front is strong? What kind of man will I be then?"

"History will tell us that Enrique Navarro understood the pain and the promise of Peru," Madison said quietly. "You're an honest and courageous man who loves his country. You're the only one who seems to doubt that."

He looked away and drew a deep breath. His face seemed to cloud over again. "Can you love your country and despise it at the same time? Can you abandon what you hate and still call yourself a patriot?"

Without knowing it, he had touched a central nerve. Madison put an arm on his shoulder and leaned her head close to his. "I've asked myself the same questions."

They sat there quietly for some time, the television blaring, the tea kettle burning on the stove. Madison wished she could see his face, somehow read his thoughts. She felt a gentle pat on her arm as he got up slowly from the sofa, his body

173

stooped, as if the full weight of Peru lay on his broad back. There was no easy answer. Perhaps there was not an answer at all.

"Good morning," Robert Little said as cheerfully as possible. He had been roused early by a Presidential aide demanding his immediate presence at Camp David. He had guessed why, and now looking at the President sitting in the breakfast room, his suspicions were confirmed. He tried a counterattack. "Good news. The papers are reporting that the price of coke has gone up on the streets and availability is down. We're hurting them."

"Down five more points in the polls this morning," the President grumbled, as if he hadn't heard Little's announcement. "The article you planted hasn't done any good. *Five points* in one day just because of rumors about this operation. What do you think would happen if it all came out?" He leaned back hard in his chair and threw his hands up helplessly. "You try to do something good for the American people, try to save a few kids from drugs and look what happens."

"Mr. President —"

President Brown silenced his Chief of Staff with a firm scowl. "Director Colby woke me up this morning. Five a.m. His Intelligence in Colombia says the head of the Cartel and members of the Shining Path's central committee met. They're sending troops into the jungle. The question is when."

"My God," the Chief of Staff said, lowering himself into a chair. "Then it's a complete loss. We can't extract them now. Not without risking a helicopter. Not without risking . . ." His words trailed off and both men were quiet for a moment.

"You got me into this, Robert, and you're getting me out." The President's voice had lost its usual calm. "You told me it would work. It didn't. Now handle it."

It crossed Little's mind that the President wasn't being quite fair. It was, after all, his hopes for re-election that had shoved the operation into high gear.

"And let me remind you," President Brown said, as if he had read Little's thoughts. "I've retained a certain amount of deniability. It's in your best interest to get this thing cleaned up."

Robert Little loosened his tie slightly and wondered why there was no air circulating in the room. He mentally reviewed his options. "We could —"

The President slammed the flat of his hand against the table, startling his Chief of Staff. "There *is* no we. You understand? You're handling this. I don't want to know. Get with Colby. Get those kids out of there, and bury this thing so goddamn deep no one will ever find it. I don't ever want to discuss it again."

A shallow section of river ran close by and occasionally, when the birds were quiet enough, Paulina could hear the water trickling over the rocks. The sound calmed her. Water always had. It offered a certain security now as well. Distant sounds were sharper near the water. And, it meant that she had a full canteen.

She had slept most of the day, then taken over watch with Rodriguez while Guzman and Vazquez dropped back to sleep with the rest of the unit. A shaft of sunlight fought its way through the thick foliage and Paulina closed her eyes and leaned her head back. It was a quiet day in the jungle.

"Hey, what's that?" Rodriguez asked suddenly.

Paulina's eyes opened and her head lifted sharply. "What?"

"That shiny thing in the sky." Rodriguez chuckled quietly.

"Cute," Paulina said, smiling.

"Hey, you think we're going home soon? I mean this place is dead, man. Ain't nothing happening here now. We kicked the shit out of them."

Paulina sat up straight, head cocked sideways, eyes closed. She had always been able to hear better with her eyes closed. One hand clasped around Rodriguez's wrist, the other was held out slightly asking for silence. "Trucks," she muttered. "Two, maybe three miles. Big ones. Radio the Captain."

Warren Moss, Mitchell Colby and Fred Nolan were waiting in the situation room when the satellite passed over the area which included the Upper Huallaga Valley of Peru and a section of jungle. From there they were able to see what the satellite saw when the satellite saw it and zero in on areas of particular interest without having to wait for still photographs.

The room looked very much like a small theater. Colby, Moss and Nolan waited on the lower level. Behind them, one level up, a row of head-phoned operators sat in front of a line of small screens and electronic equipment. "Okay," one of the operators announced, and all eyes watched the big screen intently as he punched the keys on his computer. The screen showed them the coca growing regions sloping down from the jagged mountains and running into the dense jungle. "That's the area, sir."

"There." Nolan pointed to the left hand side of the screen.

"Zoom in," Colby ordered the operator, and with one hand directed him gently. "Keep coming. More. More. That's it. Right there."

"Three flatbeds," Moss muttered.

"Bring it in a little more," Colby told the operator. "I want to know what they're carrying."

"Men," Nolan said quietly. "With rifles. Must be two hundred of them. Jesus."

"Sendero troops," Warren Moss told the Director. "And they're armed for bear."

Colby looked at Moss. "Get a cable out to SINGER right away, and put the pilots on ready. And get the President on a secure line for me."

"Singer, this is Fox. Do you read? Over." Medic Marta Guzman spoke quietly into her radio.

"Go ahead, Fox. This is Singer. Read you clear. Over," answered Harry Carson from the Lima listening post.

"Sir, Fox reports hearing several vehicles

approximately two and a half miles to the south. Can you tell us anything? Over."

Harry Carson wrinkled his eyebrows and glanced at Greg Abbott. "Have you seen the vehicles? Over."

"Negative, Singer. Permission to check it out. Over."

"Hold for orders, Fox." The printer in the van started to whine and Carson slid his chair over and read the message as it came off. *Holy shit.*

He returned to the microphone quickly. "Fox, this is Singer. You have new orders. Over."

"Go ahead, Singer. Over."

"What you heard were trucks unloading approximately two hundred armed guerrillas three miles south-southeast of your current position. Your orders are to move immediately and avoid contact. Over."

The reply did not come for a full fifteen seconds. "Copy that, Singer. Should we prepare for extraction? Over."

Harry Carson puffed out his cheeks and released air like cigarette smoke. "Negative, Fox. Not at this time. Check in next hour. I'll try to find out what's going on. Over. Singer out."

"Roger. Fox out."

"Mr. President, we've had some new developments on Maxim Two and —"

"I don't want the details, Mitchell," the President broke in sharply. "Robert's in charge of this. I don't know anything about it."

"But, Mr. President, this is critical."

"Deal with Robert Little, Mitchell. I'm a very busy man."

The line went dead and the old CIA Director slammed the receiver into the cradle. "Fucking politicians," he muttered and buzzed for his assistant. "Get me the White House Chief of Staff, pronto. And make sure the bastard's on a secure line."

His door opened and White House Chief of Staff Robert Little stepped into Colby's seventh floor office. "The bastard's right here," he said.

"Robert." Colby was shaken by his sudden appearance, and this pleased Little very much. "I assume you know the situation with Maxim Two," said the Director, turning in his desk chair and filling his coffee mug from the ever-ready pot behind him.

"The President put me in charge, Mitch," Robert Little answered, knowing his words would burn Colby. He casually lifted a framed photograph from Colby's desk and studied it for a moment. "How is the wife?"

But Colby wasn't in the mood to play. He tossed a group of photographs across his desk in Little's direction. "Satellite photos confirm our Intelligence. We've got a couple hundred guerrillas moving into the jungle. I can have the extraction underway in five or six hours."

Little sat down and thumbed through the photographs slowly. "Let's hold off on that," he answered.

Colby plowed his fist into his desk and sprang from his chair with surprising agility for a man of his age.

But Little remained seated, never looked up. "I don't think we should jump in too fast," he continued. "They probably expect that."

"Fuck what they expect," Colby roared. "I've got people in that jungle. For God's sake, Robert."

The Chief of Staff sighed heavily. "They're not just people. They're trained soldiers, Mitch. The best. You told me that yourself. Surely they can out maneuver a bunch of Peruvian terrorists."

Director Colby sat down slowly and folded his hands in his lap. "You'd better hope they can."

Robert Little frowned. "More threats, Mitch?" Colby looked away and did not answer. "It's time for us to put away our personal feelings," Little resumed. "If you can't do that then assign me someone you've cleared for Maxim. I need to watch this thing as it develops. I'll need an office with a secure line and access to all the files on Maxim One and Two."

Colby lifted the receiver on one of his desk telephones. "Warren, come to my office, please. The Chief of Staff is here. He's to be given full access to everything on Maxim."

CHAPTER FIFTEEN

They had all applied the dark green makeup to their face and necks and the backs of their hands. They moved quickly, quietly back into the heart of the jungle, keeping clear of established trails. Paulina was at point with machine gunner Robby Rodriguez a few meters back. Occasionally they circled back from opposite sides to be sure no one had picked up their trail. If they bumped into someone and could not avoid contact, their orders were to kill and kill silently.

The rest of the team was spread out in a wide

defensive line rather than single file so that it would be easier to spot the enemy before they were spotted themselves, and moving single file would beat down a path and leave tracks for the enemy to find.

They were not accustomed to moving during daylight hours, but dusk was nearing and they knew the guerrillas would bed down at night, giving them an opportunity to evaluate the enemy position and strength, then move forward again, putting more distance between themselves and the guerillas. For the first hour, while they fled their position, no one spoke. They communicated when necessary by keying their radios with prearranged signals.

The pace slowed a little in the second hour. They could afford to take more time, be more cautious. From the occasional sounds of gunfire, the enemy was nervous, jumpy, firing at anything that moved, broadcasting the fact that they were at least two hours behind. It made them all feel better to know that the enemy too was frightened, and it gave them a better sense of who the enemy was. Professional soldiers would never make so much noise, would never advertise their position. They all knew they were considerably outnumbered. But the odds were evened a bit when training and skill were factored into the equation.

Paulina and Robby made their last circle back, then caught up with the rest. "All clear, sir," Rodriguez reported. "No one's picked us up yet."

Marta Guzman had checked everyone's canteen to be sure they had not forgotten the water purification tablets in all the rush. She re-wrapped Paulina's sprains and generally made the rounds to be sure everyone was all right. She forced them to drink and eat whether they wanted food or not. No one knew when they'd have time for a break again. Her rounds made, she followed the Captain's orders and set up the 18-inch satellite dish and radio.

"Singer, this is Fox. Over."

"Fox, this is Singer. Go ahead. Over."

Guzman reported their location and asked for instructions. They all waited quietly for the reply, everyone expecting to be given a time and location to meet the helicopter. They were a couple of hours ahead of the enemy now and it seemed a good time for an extraction.

"How's your ammo holding out, Fox? Over."

"We're good, sir. Haven't expended any for a couple of days now. Over."

"Your orders are to keep moving for now. Avoid contact. Check in next hour if possible. Good luck, Fox. Singer out."

Marta Guzman quietly went about the business of tearing down the small satellite dish. Captain Vazquez cleaned his gun without a word. Paulina ate one of the MRE's and did not look up. The rest of the team said nothing. No one had to speak. They all knew. The hunters had become the hunted.

Warren Moss retrieved Robert Little from Colby's office and gave him a proud tour of what he called "his" third floor — the Operation and Situation rooms where the atmosphere was nearly as relaxed as the waiting room of a dentist's office, where personnel in casual clothes sat tensely in front of a bank of telephones and computers and chewed their fingernails while they waited for the world to end. The analysts' cubicles where bright minds with a devotion to technology and artificial Intelligence offered passionate insights into human nature. Warren Moss's office where the senior analyst himself assembled and distributed facts collected by the junior analyst, for if there was one thing in the world that Warren Moss loved beyond personal advancement, it was facts, even though he was not above stretching them when it suited his needs.

"Where are the pilots who handled the insertion?" Robert Little asked Moss. The Chief of Staff had quietly submitted to the third floor tour, then taken over Moss's office without being asked. He had demanded to know Moss's personal I.D. code for the computers and all access codes relating to Maxim. He had refused the access code issued him by CIA. He didn't want to leave any evidence of his time at CIA behind. "What's their names? Jones and Summers?"

Moss nodded. "That's right. Richard Jones and John Summers. They're on alert in Oracuza. There's a private air field there owned by one of our assets. The helicopter's hidden in a hangar."

Robert Little sat down at Moss's desk and nodded. "Who's the asset?"

Moss took a chair on the other side of his desk and realized he had never seen his office from that perspective. It felt odd, but he was pleased with the look of it overall. It was large and glassed in, with dark carpeting, and sat up on a kind of platform. From his desk he could look down on all the analysts and burrowers, lackeys and assistants. "A salesman and small-time pilot," he answered. "Rents airplanes to druggies mostly. Harry Carson, who's running communications for the jungle op in Lima, feels he's questionable at best. So we sent him on vacation till we're done. All expenses paid. Asked him where he'd like to go if he had his pick. You know what he said? Goddamn Disney World." Little chuckled and Moss resumed, "Anyway, he's having a great time and he's out of our hair."

"Good idea." Little smiled. "Get me his name." It seemed an odd request and Moss glanced up at the Chief of Staff. Little made some notes. "Maxim One is on schedule?"

"Yes, sir. It's been flawless so far. The case officer has done a terrific job. Name's McGuire and she's very good with this sort of grassroots down-in-the-dirt operation. Has a way of communicating with ordinary people. I hand-picked her myself," Moss lied. In truth he didn't like Madison very much and had not wanted her involved at all. She was a troubling, aggressive woman who had always made him feel self-conscious. "Our strategists and planners should be there in a few hours. We'll pull out the operatives we've got in there now and start phase two of the operation. Training, recruiting, weapons, etcetera."

"Good," Little answered. "Very good." He smiled and studied Warren Moss. "You're a bright young man. You've got a good future with this administration."

Moss beamed. It never occurred to him that the Administration itself might not have a future. "Thank you, sir."

"Get this message out to the Lima listening post right away."

Warren Moss took the message from the Chief of Staff. He read it over and stopped cold at the doorway. "But, sir, you can't mean —"

Robert Little stood up and removed his jacket calmly, slinging it over the back of Moss's desk chair. "Mr. Moss, do you know who I am?"

Moss swallowed and ran a hand along the side of his slick dark hair. "Of course."

"Then you know where my orders come from," Little said firmly.

"Yes, sir."

Greg Abbott sat on one of the bunks in the listening post watching Harry Carson anxiously pace the length of the van. Carson was not a tall man, five-ten perhaps, but sturdy with broad shoulders and thick forearms. His dirty blond hair was clipped close on the sides, military style, with no grey. He was, Abbott knew, at least ten years his senior and an experienced field man.

"Where the hell are they?" he demanded, knowing Abbott could not answer his question. "How long's it been since I asked Langley for an extraction? Two hours? Three?"

"One and a half," Abbott answered.

"They should know those kids can't just keep running around the fucking jungle. They need to get in position for the helicopter. What the hell's the problem?"

Abbott saw the cursor moving on Carson's computer screen and got up. "Top priority cipher coming in," he told Carson. "This must be it."

They watched the codes line up across the screen and waited for the message to decode and print out. Carson ripped the sheet from the printer. "Unbelievable," he said, sitting down in his swivel chair. "They want me to pull the plug. Cut off communication with Maxim Two. Shut the place down and take a commercial flight home. You and Madison are supposed to do the same thing as soon as the planners get here. Use escape passports, it says. *Shit.*"

Abbott jerked the message from his hand. "I don't get it."

"Politics," Carson mumbled. "The bastards."

There were three of them in all, though their masculine presence made them seem like more to Madison. She had called Enrique to join her in watching them through the security cameras at the gate when the buzzer sounded. She thought it only fitting to give him a preview of what was to come. They had pulled up in a small van. It looked new and had probably been leased at the airport. And when she opened the door for them they stood straight in their dark slacks and freshly combed hair and clean smiles. They might have been Jehovah's Witnesses out to save her soul.

The taller one with the light hair introduced himself as Johnson. The others used the names Smith and Jones and Madison was not quite clear on which was which. The names were interchangeable, as were the men. They had probably flipped for them on the drive from the airport.

187

"Mr. Navarro, sir, I'm extremely proud to shake your hand," said Johnson, stepping into the foyer with a wholesome smile. He wore a tan wind-breaker with a tie and a blue button-down shirt underneath. He had probably been over Madison's report because he seemed to know that Enrique spoke English. He didn't bother with Spanish. "This is truly an honor. We're all looking forward to working with you. What you're trying to do here is wonderful."

Smith or Jones pulled Madison aside gently while Johnson continued to compliment Enrique, and asked her to have dinner with them, while making it clear in a polite way that she was expected to leave shortly thereafter. They didn't want to get down to business right away, he explained. They wanted a relaxed atmosphere in which they could get to know one another, and they — he said they as if "they" was a single entity — thought Enrique would feel more comfortable if there was a familiar face at the table. He spoke in low reverent tones like a Priest at confession, his lips nearly touching her ear. His breath was minty and hot and he reminded Madison of a boy she had known in high school.

She saw Enrique watching while the man whispered to her even though Johnson was still singing his praises and practically doing cartwheels to keep his attention. Madison smiled and gave him a wink to let him know everything was all right. She had done her best to prepare him for what was to come, for Langley's sharp planners, Langley's sharp handlers, for others who had been trained as she had been trained. Something made her want to protect him. Perhaps counseling him would ease the guilt she'd feel if the Sendero rolled over the

Liberation Front tomorrow. Perhaps, against her best judgment, she had grown rather fond of him.

"The planners will come first," she had told him. "They'll be pink and scrubbed and you'll feel instantly as though you've known them forever. They'll love you and coddle you, romance you if you'll let them, and at the same time try every way in the world to bend you to their will. Then come the trainers to turn you into a soldier. Then the handlers to work the media. They'll have your Liberation Front looking like it's camera-ready to take over the world. They'll coach you on how to dress and they'll tell you what to say. Just remember, old boy, you're the star of the show. They can't go on if you don't like the script."

The buzzer sounded for the gate and Johnson held up a hand to let Madison know he was expecting someone. As Madison walked downstairs to look at the security screen, the one she thought was named Smith followed.

"That's him," he said. "The cook. Big guy, huh? Name's Fernando. Really knows his way around a kitchen I hear."

Madison looked at Smith for a moment then pressed the button to open the gate. Fernando lumbered back to the old light blue Chevy he drove and drove it into the compound. Fernando, Madison remembered from reading the Company's Lima files, knew his way around more than a kitchen. He had worked under the last two Lima Station Chiefs. He had taken care of quite a lot of nasty Company business. Trained as a bodyguard, his file said, which translated in Madison's mind to mean he was very good with a gun. Langley was thinking all the time, she mused. They had found a way to employ protection for Enrique in a completely nonthreatening way. He didn't have to know that the cook carried a Czech CZ-75 semi-automatic under his white jacket.

She wondered vaguely what they'd be having for dinner.

The dining room, which until now Madison had not set foot in, was in the center of the center level between the kitchen and living room. It was large and formal with doors at both ends and hand-carved trim around the walls. With the delicacy of a man half his size, Fernando had put out white napkins folded into little pyramids. He then served swordfish topped with sauteed tomatoes and scallions and a dainty tequila-lime sauce. He kept their glasses full of white wine, bowed modestly when Johnson raved about the food, and managed to not look directly at any of them.

Enrique's appetite, which had been almost non-existent for a couple of days, had returned and he seemed to be enjoying himself. Johnson and Smith and Jones were likable fellows, after all, even if they were Langley boys right down to the tips of their toes. They spoke to him of sports and Smith said he looked like an athlete. They spoke of books and Jones mentioned that Enrique seemed like a thoughtful man. They charmed him with everything they had and Enrique, with a great deal of grace let himself be courted. He even did a bit of courting himself, although they seemed unaware of being put under his spell. But Madison watched them listen to him, watched their faces relax, watched him slowly gain their attention, then their confidence, then their conviction. He asked for seconds on the food and they nearly broke their necks trying to oblige. Madison had never seen Navarro when he wasn't in one of his dark moods, never seen him shine like this. Yes, of course, she thought. This is the other side, the side that lay concealed so much of the time, the side that an English anarchist named Hilary must have loved, the side that made people flock to him like the Pied Piper, the side that had just wooed three hardened Langley boys. Enrique Navarro, she decided, would be just fine with his new keepers. He was a very fast learner.

After dinner they moved to the lower level. Madison had a game of billiards with Smith or Jones, she still was not sure, and Enrique tried out the dart board with Johnson. "Ever play chess?" she heard Johnson ask Enrique, and when he got his answer, he said he'd like to have a game one day. Madison's opponent, on the other hand, was not nearly as talkative. A very serious competitor, he had done nothing during the entire contest but march importantly around the table and scowl. Madison wasn't sure if he truly disliked her, or if it was merely an effort for him to enjoy a game with a lowly field agent. Langley insiders generally avoided the unwashed.

The buzzer sounded and Madison heard Fernando coming downstairs to have a look at the security screens. He came into the game room and whispered something into Johnson's ear. "You expecting someone named Anthony?" Johnson asked, and they all gave her a disapproving glance.

"Not expecting, actually," she said with a smile and leaned her stick against the wall. "If you'll excuse me."

She met Anthony on the front porch and knew immediately that he had come with information. Informants the world over seemed to have a certain radiance about them when there was a bit of fresh news to pass.

"It is the Sendero," Anthony told her excitedly. "They have sent many troops into the jungle to kill the Americans."

Gilberto Salaverria was thoroughly enjoying his paid vacation. The sun was bright here. It was summer and warm and Disney World was the most magnificent place he had ever seen. He wasn't sure why the Agency had sent him away, but he suspected it had something to do with the operation they were running against the traffickers, knew they wanted his airplane hangar to hide their helicopter. And what a helicopter it was. Salaverria had gotten one peep at it before they had sent him away. It was the most sophisticated flying machine he had ever seen.

The Americans thought no one knew what they were doing. He smiled at himself in the hotel room mirror as he dressed for a night on the town. The Americans had never been able to keep a secret. Salaverria had customers that would have paid a premium for what he knew if the Americans hadn't sent him away. But it had worked out. After all, he was in the United States having a great time and it had not cost him a cent.

An hour later Gilberto Salaverria was strolling through the amusement park, watching as laughing children yanked at the hands of exhausted adults, dragging them into yet another line for yet another ride. Music blared from one of a thousand loudspeakers. A burst of fireworks lit up the night sky in a spectacular display. He heard women's voices behind him and turned to see a group of young women in cut-off shorts and bikini tops. They giggled when he bowed gallantly and stepped aside for them to pass, watching their firm rumps and brown legs as they strolled by. American women always seemed acutely aware of being watched.

Salaverria had not noticed the man in the white pants and sports jacket who had followed him from the hotel. He was an older man, easy to miss, and he walked with a cane in his left hand.

Another brilliant burst of fireworks sent all eyes in the direction of the sky. Salaverria stopped briefly to admire the explosions. He felt a prick in the back of his leg, something akin to a bee sting. He slapped at the pain distractedly, then moved on.

The old man kept moving as well. He passed his victim and disappeared into the crowds, knowing his job was done. He had just used the point of his cane to introduce a single grain of Ricin into Gilberto Salaverria's blood stream. The effects were predictable. Ricin, one of the most deadly poisons available anywhere, was always fatal, always impossible to trace or cure. Within forty-eight hours Gilberto Salaverria, owner of the small Peruvian air field in Oracuza and the man that Chief of Staff Robert Little had casually inquired about, would be very dead.

CHAPTER SIXTEEN

They had moved all day when they would normally be sleeping and they were all exhausted. Their current orders were to avoid contact, maintain a purely defensive position, and it was Captain Vazquez's intention to follow those orders. He had them constantly moving deeper into the heart of the jungle. Paulina secretly questioned these tactics, believed they would have a better chance at survival if they continued their quick strike operations. Find an enemy base camp while they slept, sting and move out quietly, even the odds by slowly reducing their opposition. Continuing to move deeper into the jungle took them further away from their primary water source. Their canteens were full now but Paulina knew that they wouldn't stay that way for long. Also, hiding in the jungle presented a challenge for a unit that needed to be in a safe, defensive position. There was no high ground from which to view the enemy. Thickets and brush could provide excellent cover, but the team wanted and needed to see the enemy's avenue of approach. And this was not always possible in the jungle. Chances were, by the time they saw the enemy approaching, the enemy had seen them.

They were still moving, had been moving for hours, and the fatigue was setting in. Paulina, who normally acted as point, had spent the last hour circling back behind the team to make sure no one was trailing them. When the circle was complete, she keyed her radio to let the Captain know it was clear and Marta Guzman assembled the tiny satellite dish.

"Singer, this is Fox. Over."

They waited several seconds for a reply. None came.

"Singer, this is Fox. Come in please. Over."

After a full two minutes Guzman tried again, then looked at Captain Vazquez. "Transmitter's working normally, sir. Just can't get anyone. What do we do now?"

Vazquez's radio clicked five times. *Danger.* Paulina had spotted trouble. With one motion of the Captain's hand the team began silently spreading out in a wide circle. No one spoke. They all knew the drill.

Ten minutes later the Captain heard Paulina's whispered voice on his radio. "We've got a camp setting up about a hundred and fifty meters north of my position. That's between you and I, sir. They're within a quarter mile of you now. Over."

"How many?"

"Ten that I can see. They're building a fire. You should be able to see the light coming off ... *Shit.* Captain, I've got six, maybe eight more moving straight at me at about seventy meters. Out."

The Captain and Marta Guzman exchanged a concerned look. "Be careful Paulina," Guzman said under her breath. They could do nothing but wait now. Radio contact was impossible at this point.

Paulina saw the men nearing, counted seven of them. All armed with AK-47's, ammunition belts stretched across their chest. They walked single file, standing straight, talking casually. They would have made excellent targets. It was a relief for Paulina to see that these men were as poorly trained as the men who had guarded the processing sites.

They were closer now. She could see a cigarette package in one of their shirt pockets. She stopped breathing, used the discipline she had learned in martial arts training to make herself completely still, make herself a part of the jungle.

Ten meters. Five.

They passed so close that she felt a root under her left foot lift slightly from their weight. Willing patience on herself, she did not even turn her head to look for a full two minutes after they had passed.

"Captain, they've moved into the camp with the others. I'm on my way back, sir."

Captain Vazquez breathed a sigh of relief and crouched down next to one of his squad members, a young sergeant named Gonzales who had been pulled out of a light-fighters unit to join the team. Gonzales was lying on his stomach with his weapon positioned in front of him. His eyes never left the area he was supposed to watch as he spoke. "How you think they got so close so quick, sir?"

Vazquez patted his back reassuringly. "Don't worry. We're going to put some distance between us and them tonight. It won't happen again."

But in truth the Captain had no idea of what to expect. Had all the guerrillas entered the jungle from the south end? He wasn't sure. Was he moving away from the guerrillas or walking into more of them? He'd have to keep Paulina on point and use someone as a rear guard from now on. That left him six people with which to build an assault element if the necessity arose. But, six capable people with machine guns and grenades could still do a hell of a lot of damage.

"Seems like we could just tip on over there and take out the whole camp tonight," Gonzales said. "That would be about twenty of them we wouldn't have to worry about."

"We've got our orders, Sergeant."

"Yeah, I guess so, sir," Gonzales snorted. "Except it don't look like Singer's still listening."

* * * * *

Madison McGuire had spent half her life learning
to lie, learning to conceal emotion, and she had
gotten very good at it over the years. She prided
herself on being able to convince anyone that she
was perfectly fine while she teetered on the edge of
a complete collapse. And when a situation arose
where she felt unqualified to govern herself totally,
she generally avoided it all together and slipped
through the first crack she could find. Which was, in
fact, what she did in the case of Enrique Navarro.
She gathered up her things, called one of the
planners away quietly to let him know she was
leaving, and drove away. She didn't know how to say
good-bye to Enrique, and there was very little in the
world more horrifying to Madison than groping for
words of inspiration while someone waited
expectantly. For all that she was, Madison McGuire
was not above running when words failed her. A
cowardly act? Perhaps. But one must be brave to
commit a cowardly act entirely without fear.

The moving van had not been hard to find. She
spotted it parked in front of a two-story house with
a For Sale sign at the end of a residential street.
The back door opened and Madison climbed in. The
trailer was narrow but long and roomy. It smelled of
cigarette smoke and stale beer. Harry Carson nodded
and smiled and closed the door behind her.

"It's been a long time," he said, shaking her hand
vigorously.

Madison nodded. "Dublin, wasn't it? Six years
ago. How have you been?"

"Good till now. We've got a problem and your buddy Abbott doesn't seem to grasp it."

They walked towards Greg Abbott who had not bothered to get up. He was sitting in a swivel chair with his legs stretched out on a bunk. "Jesus, what did they do to your hair?"

Madison sat on the bunk. "Bad day?"

Abbott rubbed his eyes and sighed. "When you called earlier, I was supposed to tell you to catch the first commercial flight back to the States. We're all supposed to be pulling out of Lima right now."

Madison looked at Harry Carson then back at Abbott. "And?"

"And," Abbott repeated with no small amount of irritation, looking at Carson.

"We knew before you called that guerrillas were heading into the jungle," Carson said, pulling a cigarette from his shirt pocket. He dug for his lighter. It was old, silver and square, the kind that uses fluid. Madison saw initials engraved on the front, but they weren't Carson's. He cupped his hands around it as if he were in a wind storm, then snapped it shut. "I'm controller on the operation. Got a call from our team in the jungle hours ago. Said they heard trucks, noise. Then we got a cipher from Langley. They'd seen the guerrillas on satellite. Two hundred of them, about. So I do the natural thing and ask for an extraction location. I mean, you gotta figure we're going to pull them out. Right?" He shook his head. "Wrong. We got a top priority shriek telling us to pull the plug."

"Oh *dear*."

"We've cut the link, and it looks like we've cut them loose."

The room was quiet except for the electronic hum of the equipment. But, if the roof had blown off the van at that moment they would not have taken their eyes off each other.

How bravely we sacrifice others for flag and country, Madison thought. She had heard her father say it once. Now, suddenly, she understood fully what he had meant.

"You know," Carson said after some time. "I've seen a lot of shit but this beats all. Think I'll hang it up after this. I'm getting too old."

"Yes, well, why jump ship and leave it to the rats," Madison said thoughtfully. She too had considered leaving more than once, had even walked away fully intending not to return. But she had come back. Perhaps it was out of a sense of guilt or responsibility for what she and others like her, what the agency, the government, the whole damn human race, had made of itself. She firmly believed that if you created a monster, it was only logical that you should bear the brunt of its wretched incompetence. She reached across and pulled a cigarette from Carson's shirt pocket. "How many have to be extracted?"

"Nine at last count," Carson answered.

"Any ideas?"

Carson nodded. "The first thing I've got to do is link up with the team again. The pilots are in Oracuza. I scoped out the location before the op started. I know one of them pretty well. I think he'd work with us."

Abbott jerked forward in his chair. "Damn it, Harry. Don't you think there's a reason for all this? Come on. They didn't put us here to override their decisions. We're getting into areas where we don't belong. Do you understand what you're risking?"

Carson ignored Abbott and looked at Madison. "You willing to help out if we can come up with something?"

Madison turned to Abbott. "Perhaps this would be a good time for you to bail out, sport. If you stay, your level of knowledge goes up, you're indictable."

Abbott bent over his thighs and cupped his face in his hands tragically, as if he were watching his entire career flash before his eyes. "I'll listen," he said through his hands. "I'm not committing to anything. But I'll listen."

"Can you restore communications with our field team?" Madison asked Carson.

"Yeah. I mean, we can answer when they call, but it won't take long for Langley to figure out what's going on when we don't get on a plane home."

"Well," Madison said thoughtfully. "They deserve to be pestered a bit after this. Don't you think?"

Maxim Two had come apart and there was no putting it together again. Gilberto Salaverria, the last loose end that could not be controlled, had been disposed of quietly. Others with full knowledge of the operation were either in too deep themselves, as was the case with Mitchell Colby no matter how many times he had threatened the Chief of Staff with going public, or they understood the need for secrecy, as in the case of ambitious CIA senior analyst Warren Moss who was quickly moving towards the office of Deputy Director of Operations. Controllers, case officers and agents were easily controlled and few of them were in a position to piece it all together. The only real security problems left were the men and women who had willingly risked their lives in the jungles of Peru. Their very existence now threatened the Presidency itself, and this greatly disturbed Chief of Staff Robert Little. After all, he told himself, he was not a man entirely without conscience, he had felt the hollow stab of guilt and remorse more than once, had wanted the operation to be a success, had wanted to see team Fox come out of that jungle. And he had not enjoyed the work he had done in the last hours or the work he was about to do. But, security was paramount. He had no other options left.

He looked at the message he had just written and handed it to Warren Moss. "Get it out right away," he said gravely. "And, Warren, I don't have to tell you that anything you've been a witness to here today never leaves this office. I've been put in charge of this operation in order to protect people who are vital to this nation from being involved in something that might be misunderstood later. I don't think I have to name those people for you. Do you understand?"

Warren Moss nodded and looked down at his shoes. He understood perfectly. He understood that Robert Little was doing everything possible to cover his own ass and the President's as well, that the President had lied to the Press and now he was running scared, that Director Colby had somehow been taken out of the loop and Little had been put in his place, and he understood that the Chief of

Staff was willing to leave a group of young soldiers in the jungle to die.

"We're the protectors, Warren, you and me," Little went on. "Sometimes it's nasty work. But we have to accept the fact that this nation, this nation's image in the world, and the prestige of the office of President must be protected at all cost."

Minutes later and miles away, the Chief of Staff's message was received at a small airfield just outside the northern Peruvian city of Oracuza. The message was not signed, of course, but it bore the code that proved its authenticity.

Lieutenant Colonel Richard Jones and Captain John Summers sat on metal chairs at a card table in one of two hangars. They had been on alert for several hours, playing poker to pass the time, waiting for the order to come. Neither one of them had been particularly happy about flying the big Pave Low deep-penetration helicopter through secured airspace to get to the jungle, but they were willing and able. The order they had just received, however, was not at all what they had expected.

****TOP SECRET****
****CODE LH2139****
ABORT MISSION AT ONCE. POSSIBLE SECURITY BREACH. IMPOSSIBLE TO CONTINUE UNDER CURRENT AIRSPACE RESTRICTIONS. RETURN TO U.S. SOUTHERN COMMAND IN PANAMA

A.S.A.P. BLACK CODE RULES. END TRANSMISSION

"Black code rules," Richard Jones muttered, reading over the transmission for the third time. "They want us to fly out of here without logging a flight plan, without an okay from the government, without collision lights, but they won't risk us flying over the jungle. Something very weird is going on."

"You don't think —"

John Summers was quickly interrupted. "No way." The Colonel shook his head seriously. "They must have other plans. I don't know. I don't get it. We're better equipped than anyone."

"We should count our blessings. Panama's one step closer to home." Summers cocked his head towards the helicopter. "I'll check her out, get things ready. You want to check the weather?"

"Weather's clear," Richard Jones said distractedly. He was still staring at the latest transmission from Langley. "We'll be outta here before daylight."

They had been moving nonstop for several hours now. With five hours until dawn, they'd put a good three miles between them and the last enemy camp. Paulina had moved ahead as usual and Captain Vazquez had sent Gonzales back as rear guard. The Captain wanted no more surprises.

Paulina was more than a mile ahead of the team, moving quickly but cautiously. She was tired. Too tired. She had caught herself drifting off once when she stopped for water. She didn't want to stop again. Movement stimulated mind and body.

There was a small village just ahead on their maps, and Vazquez wanted to get past it before they stopped to rest. Paulina had just seen the first faint glow of light from the village when she heard the sound. Very soft. She closed her eyes for a second. Which direction had it come from? Perhaps it was just the breeze, a branch brushing . . .

Sound again. Distinctly human this time. The low murmur of voices. She keyed her radio five times. *Danger*. The jungle was dense here. It was hard to see . . .

There. Three hundred meters northeast. Movement. They were walking in no particular formation from the direction of the village. They carried rifles and there were more of them than she could accurately count from her position.

"Captain, I've got armed guerrillas and they're heading in your direction. I can't see well enough from here to get an accurate count. Maybe forty or fifty."

Vazquez hadn't counted on this, hadn't expected the guerrillas to move at night. He looked at his team. They were too tired to continue running at a reasonable pace. Even though his orders were to avoid contact, there was a confrontation coming, and Vazquez wanted to be on the winning end of it. He knew he had the advantage here, had surprise on his side, had a group of trained soldiers who knew what to do. The assault would be loud. Paulina was the only one with a silenced weapon. The enemy camps they had passed were all sleeping. They would hear the noise but it would be difficult for them to pinpoint the direction. And, as far as he knew, the enemy wasn't carrying radios. They couldn't contact another unit for help. Why not let them walk right into a trap and even the odds a little? If everything went according to plan, they could neutralize half the threat in the first few seconds.

Vazquez spoke quietly into his radio. "Holgodo, stay ahead of them and let me know every chance you get what's going on. How long do we have?"

"Twenty-five, thirty minutes, sir."

"Okay people," Vazquez ordered. "Let's set up a defensive perimeter. Dig in as deep as you can. We don't want to give them a target. You all know your areas of responsibility. Get in position. *Go.*" He spoke into his radio again. "Gonzales, head back on the double."

The team moved quickly, spreading out in the shape of a half moon, M-16's raised, resting against their shoulders, ready to be switched to firing position. Machine-gunner Robby Rodriguez set up his big gun on its tripod. Marta Guzman got the grenade launcher into position.

Paulina Holgodo raced ahead through a small clearing, keeping a hundred meters ahead of the enemy. She waited in the heavy brush to count them as they entered the clearing. There were considerably fewer than she had originally estimated. This concerned her at first, but there was no evidence that they had broken off and split up, no movement that she could detect in either direction. It would have been inconsistent with the way the enemy had performed so far anyway. Why would they begin to take precautions that they hadn't bothered with before?

She spoke quietly into her radio. "Captain, there's not as many of them as I thought. I count twenty-eight going through a little clearing. They've got AK's and a few grenades on their belts. They're traveling in groups of four now. Kind of spread out and disorganized. Doesn't look like it'll be a problem . . . Uh oh, Captain. Looks like one of them has a radio and he's talking to someone. Keep your eyes open, sir. I could have missed something."

Twelve minutes later Vazquez heard two clicks. He whispered into his radio. "Okay people, Paulina's coming in. Keep your weapons in the safety position. I don't want any accidents. Take your goggles off once she's in. We need time for our eyes to adjust."

Paulina suddenly appeared in the display on Rodriguez's goggles. She was slightly crouched, moving quickly, side-stepping roots and reeds with astounding agility. Rodriguez smiled his appreciation. "Scout's coming in, Captain," he reported into his radio. "Fifteen meters to the northeast." No one heard her, and even with the night vision equipment, only two team members detected movement in the goggles' green display.

"They've found their footing and picked up speed a little, sir," Paulina said, once she found the Captain. Her breathing was hard, but she was wide awake now. They all were. "We've got ten minutes at the most."

The Captain nodded. "Get into position."

Paulina took the northeast corner a few meters

from Rodriguez. She had the only silenced weapon and hopefully she could fire into the first two groups as they approached before the others realized what was happening. They all had certain areas where they would concentrate their fire. It made for an organized ambush, expended less ammunition and reduced the chance of one of the team getting hit by friendly fire.

They heard the rustle of tree branches.

Vazquez keyed in the danger signal. All weapons were quickly switched to firing position.

Paulina saw them first, two small groups of four walking within ten meters of one another. She concentrated on the group to the right and gently wrapped her finger around the trigger of the silenced H&K MP5 submachine gun. Just a little closer, she thought. *Closer. Closer. Fifty meters. Forty. Now.*

The quiet barrage of bullets dropped the first four immediately. The group walking next to them turned instinctively towards the sound of their friends' bodies hitting the ground. They seemed to freeze for a moment. Two other groups appeared from behind. Then the loud brilliant flash of Robby Rodriguez's machine gun dropped six of the guerrillas instantly.

The others scattered to find cover, unknowingly running right into the area covered by the rest of the team. The jungle was suddenly blindingly bright with the white-blue tracers from the M-16's. One of the guerrillas managed to pull a grenade from his belt, but Rodriguez got him in mid-throw and as the grenade exploded at his feet it was a sight they would never forget.

Then quiet. Paulina snapped her goggles into place. No movement. The ambush had barely lasted a full twenty seconds.

"Check it out," the Captain ordered. The rest of the team stayed in position while Paulina and Gonzales left their post to inspect the damage.

They counted the bodies without emotion. Right now they felt only the exhilaration of emergency, of combat, of survival. Later the remorse, the horror, the fear and anxiety of post-combat shock would set in. It always did. But now, emotion was a luxury they could not afford.

"Captain," Gonzales reported. "Got all of them, sir. But only one radio. They weren't talking to each other. Must be others in the area."

The team would have some warning. The guerrillas had not mastered their jungle skills. They made a good deal of noise moving in, but it wasn't much help.

Holgodo and Gonzales exchanged one quick look when they heard the shots. Paulina knew what had happened. So did Gonzales. She had not miscounted earlier. The guerrillas had simply broken off, separated, began looping each other's trails, apparently communicating by radio. It was smart. If they encountered any enemy, they would have already surrounded them. Paulina, Vazquez, all of them had underestimated the Sendero troops. It would prove to be a very costly mistake.

The team had no time to prepare, to select decent firing positions. No time to plan, to dig in. They had moved when they heard the noise, but it wasn't enough. The guerrillas had already started firing from behind them. From his position just behind the team's line and center, Captain Vazquez was most vulnerable. He took several rounds in the chest. Three more members went down with him before they could get into position.

Robby Rodriguez managed to get turned around and open fire. The man next to him yelled and rolled backwards when a bullet exploded into his face. Rodriguez screamed an obscenity and began wildly hosing the area with his machine gun, eyes wide, tears streaming down his face.

Paulina and Gonzales had made it back. Paulina leveled her submachine gun and let off several short bursts. Gonzales had his M-16 pressed against his shoulder, spraying whatever moved.

On the extreme northwest corner of the team's defensive line, Marta Guzman positioned the grenade launcher and fired into the area where the most light was coming from. Careful aiming was a waste of time at this point. Night vision was now practically nonexistent with light blazing from so many weapons.

The grenade exploded dead center of the attackers. Gonzales, Holgodo and Rodriguez moved in to finish off what was left of the enemy. The sound, the screams of rage, of pain, the light, the confusion was unlike anything they had ever experienced. The guerrillas had lost a total of forty-six men, but it had cost the team more than fifty percent of its initial strength, had cost them the man they looked to for orders, for advice, the man they had trusted to get them out of the jungle alive. It had cost them the friends they had made and thought they'd keep for life. It had cost them their faith.

Gonzales sat on the ground next to the Captain's

body, sobbing quietly, his head pressed against the Captain's chest. Paulina and Guzman and Rodriguez looked on helplessly, fighting back their own fear and grief.

Marta Guzman touched Gonzales' shoulder gently. "The Captain's dead. We've got to move." She grabbed one of his arms to help him up but he flung it free. "We can't stay here, Jorge," she insisted.

"What's the fucking point?" he asked, turning his dirty tear-streaked face to her. "We're all dead anyway, man."

They all understood what he was feeling, all struggled with the same fears, all wondered if they'd get home again.

Rodriguez ranked them, and even in the face of his own monumental terror, he did what any good soldier would do. "Move your ass, Gonzales, and act like a soldier. That's an order. I'm taking command of this unit. We're getting out of this shithole with or without you. You in or out?"

Gonzales wiped a sleeve across his face and nodded. "I'm in," he said, rising slowly and picking up his weapon. "I'm in."

They gathered up what extra ammunition they could carry without it slowing them down and moved immediately. Enemy forces would move in soon, they knew. There was no time to grieve for the ones they had to leave behind.

After an hour of winding through the dense jungle at top speed, they stopped to radio in. "Singer, this is Fox. Come in. Over," Marta Guzman said into her radio. Her voice was weak, shaky. She muttered to herself, "Be there, Singer. Please be there."

In the Lima listening post, Harry Carson leapt from his chair when he heard the voice. He hit the switch on his radio and leaned towards the microphone. "Fox, this is Singer. I've got you loud and clear. Over."

Marta Guzman reported their position. "Singer, we're in trouble. We've reduced enemy strength by forty-six, but we lost the Captain and half the unit. Requesting extraction as soon as possible, sir. Over."

"My God," Madison said, moving closer to the radio, putting a hand on Carson's shoulder. Abbott stood next to her, staring blankly at the equipment.

"What's your strength now, Fox? Over," Carson asked.

"Gonzales, Rodriguez, Holgodo and me," Guzman answered. "We're outnumbered pretty bad, sir."

Carson looked at Madison. "Jesus, there's only four of them left. They'll never make it."

"Stall them," Madison said. "And keep them calm, Harry. If they suspect they've been cut loose, they'll panic."

Carson spoke into his radio again with as much calm as he could muster. "We're holding for an extraction point now, Fox. We'll have it in a couple of minutes. Don't worry. We're gonna get you out of there."

Madison turned to the satellite map on the wall and located the team's current position. She ran her finger up a line that ran near the river to a large clearing. "What's this?" she asked.

"The State Department bulldozers have been clearing there," Abbott said. "There's room for a helicopter to sit down."

"This looks like the only option," she told Carson,

pointing out the spot on the map. "If they can make it that far, maybe we can figure something out."

Carson keyed his microphone. "Fox, we've got your extraction point." He gave them the location. "It's approximately twelve miles northeast of your present location. Are you in good enough shape to make it there by twenty-two hundred? Over."

They waited for the reply, knowing the team was looking over their maps, talking it over. Finally Guzman came in again. "We'll be there, sir. Over."

"Okay, Fox, listen to me. We've been experiencing some communication and equipment failures. But the extraction's on no matter what. You copy?"

"We copy that, sir. Over."

"Be careful, Fox. Singer out."

Madison sat down on the edge of a table and lit a cigarette without speaking. Abbott had fallen into his swivel chair. His heel tapped nervously against the metal bottom.

"Jesus," Carson muttered. "I can't believe I just did that."

"They needed something to hold on to," Madison said quietly. "We'll do what we can to make it so."

Abbott had walked his chair to the computer. He typed something and studied the screen. "We can probably get a private plane to Oracuza. I don't see any regular commercial flights scheduled."

Carson pressed a number into the secure telephone and spoke after a short wait. "Rich, it's Harry Carson. I'll be there in a few hours. We need to talk."

"Sorry," answered Lieutenant Colonel Richard Jones from the small airfield in Oracuza. "Got orders to clear out. We're packing it up now."

"We've got four people left in the jungle and a couple hundred Sendero troops closing in," Carson said. "Langley or Washington or some sons of bitches in between decided to leave them there."

Jones glanced at his navigator John Summers. "Why?"

"Someone got scared and pulled the plug is my guess," Carson answered. "We've got to get them out, Rich."

"I hope you're not talking about what I think you're talking about," Jones said. "I've had a good career, Harry, and I'm looking forward to my pension and my rocking chair. Besides, it's just me and John Summers here now. Everyone else is gone. We don't even have anyone to work the mini-guns."

"I'm bringing help with me," Carson said.

"Now just a minute, Harry," Jones said. "I've got orders."

"You've been in-country," Carson said quietly. "You know what it's like. Those kids have lost half their unit and their command. They're scared to death. We can't leave them to die."

"What the hell will I tell Langley?"

"You're a clever guy," Carson said. "Make something up."

CHAPTER SEVENTEEN

At CIA headquarters in Langley, Virginia, Warren Moss sat outside the Director's seventh floor office waiting for the okay to go in. Gretchen, Colby's assistant, a formidable woman with steel grey hair who was generally known to be Colby's watchdog, nodded Moss curtly into the Director's office.

"I know you're busy, sir. I'm sorry to bother you. It's just that I'm concerned about what's going on with our Peruvian operations. The Chief of Staff is out of control —"

"Warren," the Director interrupted, pushing his chair away from his desk and standing. "Maxim Two belongs to Robert Little now. The President took us out of it. I don't like it either." He walked over to the window, one hand jingling the change in his pocket. "He'll realize he's out of his league and we'll clean up the mess. We'll get our people out."

"We may not have any people left by then."

Colby turned towards Moss. "What are you talking about?"

"He shut down the listening post and ordered the pilots back to Panama," Moss answered.

"Are you positive?"

"No doubt," Moss answered. "I've watched him step by step."

Colby sat down behind his desk and rubbed his forehead. *Jesus Christ.*"

"You've got to do something."

Colby nodded. "The problem is, what can we do without directly disobeying a presidential order?"

"Maybe the President doesn't know what his Chief of Staff is up to."

"Doubtful." Colby reached for his telephone. "Get me the President on a secure line, pronto."

The reply came from his assistant a few minutes later. "The President . . . uh . . . can't take your call right now."

Colby slammed the phone in its cradle and looked at Moss. It wasn't often a President refused a call from the Director of the largest Intelligence gathering agency in the world. "I guess that rules out using official channels. The President's cut himself off completely."

"Mr. Colby." It was the voice of his assistant again. "There's something from the cipher room here for Warren."

"Bring it in," Colby ordered.

The woman appeared and handed Moss the decoded message. He read it and looked at the Director.

"Everything that's coming in from Peru is funneled through me before Little sees it. I'm not sure what to make of this. A search of flight records doesn't show any of our people on flights out of Lima under any of the names we've got listed for them."

The old Director puckered his lips and leaned back in his chair. "What about the pilots?"

Moss shook his head. "Nope. Engine trouble with the Pave Low."

Colby folded his big hands in his lap. His eyes narrowed slightly and his face crinkled into a thousand wrinkles. It was a nice smile, Moss thought, although he wasn't quite sure what the Director had found so amusing.

They had traveled another five miles by sunup, moving as quickly and quietly as their fatigued bodies would allow. Paulina was slightly ahead of the rest, but only by a few meters. They stayed closer now that there were only the four of them, keeping within visual range of one another but with enough distance between so that one burst from enemy fire wouldn't wipe them out.

All of them were experiencing severe post-combat shock, and now their extensive training was paying off. They had moved without conversation, moved automatically, assumed a position, an area of responsibility, and stuck with it.

They dozed for an hour just before dawn, then moved on again, knowing the enemy was well-rested, knowing the hunters would move quickly in daylight, knowing they had to reach the extraction point and dig in. That objective was the only thing that kept them going.

The trip to Oracuza had only taken a few hours from beginning to end. Anthony had come through once again and found them a pilot with a four-seater who flew them straight to the airfield, quietly refueled and took his payment without question. He was in the air again a half hour after landing.

Lieutenant Colonel Richard Jones, Harry Carson, Madison and Abbott went over the plan for the night, studying their most recent charts and satellite maps, while Captain Summers went through the lengthy process of checking and double-checking every piece of equipment on the helicopter.

"What if there's trouble and we can't land?" Abbott asked.

"With the guns on that baby putting out about a hundred and fifty rounds a second," Carson said, "we could sit down anywhere."

"Is everyone okay with the machine guns in the Pave Low?" Jones asked.

"Not a problem," Madison said, still studying the map.

"I've got a thirty-eight at home," Abbott said lamely.

"I'll show you how they work," Carson told him. "It's no big thing. They shoot tracers out like fire. Just follow the stream. It's kind of like a video game."

Right, Abbott thought, a video game that kills.

"Okay," Jones said. "Madison, you'll take the rear position on the left-side cargo door. Harry, you take the front-side right. Greg, you'll take the rear gun next to Harry."

He looked at Abbott for a moment. "Ever seen combat before, son?" Abbott shook his head. Jones rested a big hand on his shoulder and gave him a reassuring wink. His brown eyes gleamed with heroic light, withdrawing into a past none of them had been a part of. "I have. Plenty of times. This is just a Sunday drive. We go in, come back to refuel, and it's off to Panama. No big deal. They call me Night Stalker. You know why? Cause I could get that bird in and out of a tree notch in the dead of night without even shaking a leaf loose."

"We don't want to hear about your sex life, Rich." Carson laughed and started towards the helicopter.

Jones grabbed the baseball cap lying on the table and pulled it onto his head. "Ooh, I love it when you talk dirty," he said, running after him. He wrapped an arm around Carson's shoulder and made a few smacking noises for effect.

"Brave guys, huh?" Abbott said.

Madison chuckled. "Listen to them, Abbott. They're talking about their penises. They're scared half to death."

"Are you?"

Madison looked at Abbott, at the valiant face he had put on for them all, at the anxious eyes, and for a moment there was a kind of lapse as if her cover story had suddenly faded from memory. She realized unhappily that she had forgotten Abbott along the way, forgotten his fear, the dread he must be feeling. "A British author once said that there's no such thing as bravery — only degrees of fear. I believe that. We're all afraid in our own way. Afraid of dying, of living, afraid of love."

She wavered, picked up a pencil from the table and studied it for a moment. "Listen, Abbott, I wouldn't risk my life with someone I thought couldn't make the mark. I've never questioned that about you. The anticipation's the worst thing. Just take it minute by minute."

Abbott nodded gravely. "Why do you do this, Madison? I mean, isn't there something else you want to do?"

"Always wanted to touch the tip of my tongue to my nose, but that's —"

"Seriously," Abbott insisted.

In truth she was doing exactly what she had always wanted to do. There had never been any question in her mind about her destiny. Her father had traveled this path and she had studiously planned to follow him into the Agency when she was still a child rehearsing her future by peering round corners at the neighbors and eavesdropping on telephone extensions.

She smiled. "Serious are you? Never known a controller who didn't take himself too bloody serious."

From the rear of the hangar they heard Richard Jones' voice calling for them. Madison looked at Abbott. "Zero hour, old boy. Shall we go, then?"

Robert Little had been sitting in the seventh floor reception area for nearly ten minutes waiting to see the Director. Colby had anticipated his arrival and made prior arrangements with his assistant. The Chief of Staff had tried to bully himself past the stout Gretchen, but with the Director's full approval, she had wedged herself between the Chief of Staff and Colby's door and did not budge until he had taken his seat. Little was furious, of course, but Colby thought it might do him good to stew for a while. When he was allowed into the office, Director Colby was turned away and pouring himself a cup of coffee from the pot behind his desk.

"Mitchell, I demand to know what's going on." He was speaking to the Director's back.

Colby calmly added milk to his cup and then turned slowly. "What's the problem, Robert? Did it get away from you?"

"Your people aren't pulling out. I ordered them to pull out and no one's moving."

Colby took a sip from his coffee. His pale eyes glistened at Little over the mug. "Correction, Robert. They're *your* people now. Remember?"

The Chief of Staff grew very still, even the twitch had left his eye. He looked at Colby for quite some time before he spoke. "You're finished, Mitch."

Colby set his mug down slowly. "You know, Robert, as long as I have the pleasure of taking you with me, I just don't give a shit."

Pleasurably, he watched the Chief of Staff leave his office in a fury. Then he buzzed Warren Moss. "Get hold of the base commander at U.S. Southern Command in Panama. If I'm right, we've got people coming in from Peru tonight and he'll have to be notified. I don't care what you have to tell him. I want medical personnel there to meet the helicopter in case we have wounded. Our people are to be put on a military transport to Andrews quietly and *safely*. Top secret V.I.P treatment. If anything happens to those people after they hit Panama, tell him I'll chew a ring around his ass so big he'll fall through."

They had four people, three M-16's, one silenced MP5, one grenade launcher, and a flare. It would have to do. They had reached the extraction point with two hours to spare and gotten busy digging in as best they could, rigging wire to grenade pins then winding the wires through the trees. If the enemy wanted to break through the tree line directly in front of the team's position, they'd have to pay the price. Of course, most of them would get through, but by then the confusion would be absolute, and that if nothing else would slow them down. The team had positioned themselves within fifteen meters of one another, their backs to the river, dug in on a sloped bank of wet reeds and foliage. No one could get behind them this time unless they came by boat.

They had managed to go all day without a confrontation, moving slowly and quietly, using the avoid-and-evade tactics they had all learned. They'd seen the remnants of several enemy camps and out-maneuvered a column of fifty guerrillas. But the enemy was becoming more skilled at picking up trails. They were learning from past mistakes just like any soldier would. And they were moving into the area. There was no doubt about that.

Gonzalez spoke into his radio. "Batteries just gave out on my goggles. Can't see dog shit past the tree line. Anybody got any extra."

"Negative," Paulina answered.

"Sorry," Guzman said.

"Don't worry, Gonzales. You'll know when the shit starts," Rodriguez added.

"Got movement," Paulina whispered. "At twelve o'clock. Fifty, sixty meters beyond the tree line."

They all switched their weapons to firing positions.

One of the grenades exploded. The area was briefly illuminated. There were screams, men running. Then the hollow cracks of what sounded like a hundred AK-47's and white light blazing from their muzzles along the tree line.

"They don't see us yet," Rodriguez told his radio. "They're just freakin'. Hold fire, everyone. Wait for my order. We don't want to give up our position yet."

*　*　*　*　*

It was not a comfortable flight. The Pave Low plunged over the Andes, rising and dipping along the mountain range, barely clearing the ground at times. Carson, Madison and Abbott sat on a floor panel in the rear of the helicopter, straps holding them in place, backs pressed against metal.

Carson smiled and patted Abbott's knee. "Like a ride at Six Flags, isn't it."

Up front, Richard Jones spoke to his co-pilot. "How's the sys check."

"We're in good shape," John Summers reported. "Everything's working."

Jones spoke into his headset again. "ETA five-zero minutes, people. Better get unstrapped and find your legs."

Madison was up first. She grabbed a helmet and put it on over the tiny headsets they all wore, carefully buckling the chin strap. Abbott and Carson followed suit and moved close to their assigned positions.

"Four minutes," Jones reported. "Get the doors open."

Guns were mounted on cargo doors on each side of the big aircraft. Carson and Abbott took one side, Madison took the other. They released the door levers at the same time. The doors slid open with a rumble and the sound and the air rushed in the helicopter, assaulting their senses like a wind tunnel.

"Where's that fucking helicopter?" Guzman muttered to herself.

Another wire was tripped. Another explosion. The

horrible shrieks of men dying. Then more shooting, wildly, in no particular direction. Rodriguez wondered how many had been lost to their own friendly fire.

Suddenly, several guerrillas broke through the line at sixty meters to the left front of the team's position.

"Paulina," Rodriguez ordered. "*Do it.*"

The MP5 was not only silenced, it had no muzzle flash. Paulina pressed her knees against the bank, lifted her upper body slightly and trained the submachine gun on the approaching enemy.

Then, another grenade exploded and seconds behind the explosion, more guerrillas broke through. Then two more grenades went off and the area was suddenly ablaze in light and fire.

They couldn't wait any longer, Rodriguez realized. They'd have to compromise their position and fight back before the enemy got closer. "*Go,*" he ordered, knowing they couldn't hold them off for long. There were too many of them.

Rodriguez, Gonzales and Paulina opened up their weapons at the same time. Marta Guzman aimed the grenade launcher at the tree line and fired.

"Oh, *man,*" Jones saw the explosion from the air. "Stand to, guns," he ordered. "For the unwashed that means get your ass ready, people. ETA one-zero minutes. And we got ourselves a fire fight down there."

In the rear, Madison watched the activity over the sight of the gun she had tilted towards the ground. She yelled to Carson. "They're backed up to the river, I think. Appears to be the smallest concentration there."

Carson nodded. "I can't see shit from where I am right now."

"Twenty seconds," Jones reported.

"Ready," Carson answered, hitting his mic.

"Ready," Madison said.

"Ready," Abbott added, and felt a rush of adrenaline surge at top speed through his body.

Lieutenant Colonel Richard Jones studied the ground through the infrared display and started the descent in a slow spiral. The quiet throbbing of the silenced tail rotors allowed the Pave Low to remain virtually undetected until it was just overhead.

Madison saw it from her side first, the bright flashes of rifle fire coming from the darkness below. She aimed the mounted mini-gun in the direction of the flashes and let off several short bursts. The light and the noise and the vibration from the gun nearly threw her backwards.

The helicopter rotated again. Madison heard Carson firing from the other side of the chopper, but she did not take her eyes off the ground.

Abbott put his sights on an area in the trees where there was a heavy concentration of flashes and squeezed the trigger. He held it down, spraying the area, expending nearly four thousand rounds before he let up. He was more afraid than he had ever been in his life.

The nose tilted up slightly and the helicopter hovered at about two and a half feet off the ground. "*Shit,*" Carson yelled, when he saw the spark from a bullet bounce off the rim of the cargo door a foot from his head.

"Jesus," Abbott yelled, but no one heard him. No one could hear anything now but the loud reports from the helicopter's machine guns and bullets from AK-47's pinging off the helicopter.

Madison picked up a loaded M-16 and slung it across her chest, then leaned out the cargo door and waved an arm for the team. It took her a moment to see them. Her eyes were still fighting to recover from the brilliant blue flashes of the mini-gun. The team rose up quickly, four black shadows against the night, and started the run towards the chopper.

"Madison." It was Carson's voice yelling into his mic. "Behind us."

She spun the M-16 around in the direction of the tail rotor and saw three men firing, running in their direction. They had gotten within twenty yards. Madison let off a burst and cleared the area. Gonzales and Guzman hurled themselves through the cargo door and tumbled into the helicopter.

Madison saw two other team members approaching slowly from a few yards away. One or both of them was hurt.

"I need someone on this side," Madison yelled to Carson. "We've got wounded. Cover me."

She jumped from the chopper and ran to the two soldiers. One had a leg wound. She wrapped her arm around his waist and helped the other soldier walk him to the chopper.

The noise had nearly subsided. She heard a few pings against the side of the aircraft, then heard Abbott let off a short burst.

Then an unearthly quiet. So sudden. So eerie. She helped Rodriguez and Holgodo into the helicopter and hit the switch on her mic. "All accounted for, Colonel."

"Not too soon for me," Jones answered from the front. "We're outta here."

Once the helicopter had lifted up and the cargo doors were shut, they turned from their positions to examine their passengers. Carson looked at Abbott and held his hand up for a high-five. "All *right,*" he said. "Good job, Abbott."

Greg Abbott's knees seemed to give slightly. He slid down the wall into a heap on the floor. His eyes were wide open, a bit glazed.

Guzman and Gonzales had said nothing. They sat quietly with their backs against the inside of the helicopter, weapons resting between their knees, Gonzales with one teardrop on his cheek. The rest he held inside him. Madison could only guess what they'd been through, what they'd seen.

She checked Rodriguez's leg and Carson helped apply some first aid from the kit in the chopper. Rodriguez had passed out, either from the pain or from exhaustion, Madison wasn't sure which, but his breathing seemed to be regular. Paulina was sitting next to him with a hand on his arm.

Madison smiled. "He'll be fine. It's not serious. Name's Madison McGuire. You okay?"

Paulina nodded and shook Madison's hand. "Paulina Holgodo. Nice to meet you, McGuire."

EPILOGUE

Associated Press, Huancayo: *In the heart of Peru's breadbasket department of Junin, the Sendero Luminoso, or Shining Path, is locked in a battle for dominance with the newly formed National Liberation Front. The Shining Path, a neo-Maoist guerilla organization, developed from an extremist splinter group of the Peruvian communist Party, has been conducting urban terrorist operations and rural guerrilla warfare in Peru with the objective of overthrowing the democratically elected government in Peru since the 1980s. But National Liberation Front forces, which have been recently attracting an enormous amount of popular support from Peru's peasants and Quechua Indians, continue to push the Shining Path back towards the mountains. The sudden success of the National Liberation Front is due in part to its charismatic leader, Enrique Navarro, a farmer turned rebel, and in part to a new infusion of resources. Finances for the organization to date remain a mystery . . .*

It was evening in Georgia, a July evening, and Madison rode with the windows down listening to the hum of the engine, the quiet of a warm southern night. She was going home at last, to her sanctuary, home to the shelter she'd bought as protection from the world. But no place was far enough now, no place remote enough to forget Peru. She thought of the boy who had tried to rob her at Plaza San Martin. His wide, dark eyes smoldered in her memory like a brush fire. His eyes had so much behind them that day, too much for her comfort, and she looked into them again now as she drove. The faces of Peru would be forever etched in her mind.

She entered the small town of Helen and parked at Langford's General Store. She thought of the old Director, remembered the day he'd said good-bye, the day he announced that his resignation had been accepted by the President. The world had changed, he had told a group in the Company dining room, the CIA needed new blood. No one knew then that Mitchell Colby had one last mission to perform for his country. No one could have known that the old

Cold Warrior would soon violate one of the pledges he and his agency had always held most sacred, the oath of secrecy.

It was quite a story. The source, the newspapers reported, was a high level unnamed official at CIA. But, Madison knew, as the others at Langley knew, the story had been Colby's swan song, and they all watched with a great deal of awe as the mighty quickly fell victim to their own conspiracies. The White House was practically under siege. Telephone calls and letters rolled in by the thousands demanding the truth. Had Chief of Staff Robert Little and the President of the United States really conspired to leave young Americans for dead in the jungles of Peru just to protect their re-election hopes? The Press was going after them with the kind of enthusiasm that had not been seen since Iran-Contra.

The *Washington Post* reporter who first broke the story was refusing to name his source. Some members of Congress were demanding a special investigation into the entire operation. But even without proof, without an investigation or an admission of guilt, the damage was done. The President's popularity had dropped so far in the polls that he had no chance of climbing out again. Colby's story, Colby's song, had changed the course of the nation. And Madison was sorry to see him go.

She climbed out of the car and walked into Langford's. Mrs. Langford was bent over the counter impatiently flipping through the pages of a magazine. The fat on the underside of her arms jiggled with the turn of each page. She was wearing a bright floral dress with no sleeves. Madison smiled. "Well, then, Mrs. Langford. I trust your summer's been pleasant so far."

Mrs. Langford looked up with a good deal of surprise at seeing Madison standing at her counter, and Madison realized that her surprise was at the tone of Madison's voice. She had never actually tried to engage the woman in friendly conversation, had never been particularly interested in her new neighbors at all. But today, on her first day home, Mrs. Langford and the residents of Helen, Georgia seemed like something to be cherished.

"It's hot," Mrs. Langford muttered, in the voice that let everyone know that she had quite a lot to complain about. "You been out of state?"

Madison found a cart and tossed in a few items. "Out of the country, actually. It's almost winter where I've been."

"Winter in July," Mrs. Langford said with a shake of her head. She had come from behind the counter and was following Madison while she did her shopping. She reached inside Madison's cart and picked up a box of laundry soap, replaced it on the shelf and tossed in another. "This one's a better deal. Where did you say you'd been? Europe somewhere?"

"Peru," Madison answered. She had wondered how long it would take Mrs. Langford to get around to that.

"Is it pretty there?"

Madison handed her something from her bag and watched while Mrs. Langford carefully unwound the string and tissue paper. It was the doll she'd bought from the street vendor in Lima. She hadn't known then exactly why she'd bought it. "Thought you'd like a souvenir."

Mrs. Langford's stern face softened for a moment. She looked at the doll, then at Madison. It was the first time Madison had seen her entirely without words and she ventured to save her. "Been collecting mail for me? Anything important?"

Mrs. Langford stepped behind her counter where she was once again untouchable. "I don't read it. I just sort it out."

"Haven't put steam to it yet, have you?" Madison asked, smiling. With a bit of direction, Mrs. Langford might have made a better spy than half the lot from Langley.

"You've got a visitor," Mrs. Langford said, and her voice took on a distinct and familiar tone of disapproval. "That singer. I swear, with all that money you'd think she could afford a decent pair of jeans."

Minutes later Madison pulled onto the dirt lane that led to the house, saw the rented automobile in the drive, saw Dani on the porch waving. She smiled. There were rewards for survival.

A few of the publications of
THE NAIAD PRESS, INC.
P.O. Box 10543 • Tallahassee, Florida 32302
Phone (904) 539-5965
Mail orders welcome. Please include 15% postage.

HAPPY ENDINGS by Kate Brandt. 272 pp. Intimate conversations
with Lesbian authors.   ISBN 1-56280-050-7 $10.95

THE SPY IN QUESTION by Amanda Kyle Williams. 256 pp. 4th
spy novel featuring Lesbian agent Madison McGuire.
                                         ISBN 1-56280-037-X   9.95

SAVING GRACE by Jennifer Fulton. 240 pp. Adventure and
romantic entanglement.   ISBN 1-56280-051-5   9.95

THE YEAR SEVEN by Molleen Zanger. 208 pp. Women surviving
in a new world.   ISBN 1-56280-034-5   9.95

CURIOUS WINE by Katherine V. Forrest. 176 pp. Tenth
Anniversary Edition. The most popular contemporary Lesbian
love story.   ISBN 1-56280-053-1   9.95

CHAUTAUQUA by Catherine Ennis. 192 pp. Exciting, romantic
adventure.   ISBN 1-56280-032-9   9.95

A PROPER BURIAL by Pat Welch. 192 pp. Third in the Helen
Black mystery series.   ISBN 1-56280-033-7   9.95

SILVERLAKE HEAT: A Novel of Suspense by Carol Schmidt.
240 pp. Rhonda is as hot as Laney's dreams.   ISBN 1-56280-031-0   9.95

LOVE, ZENA BETH by Diane Salvatore. 224 pp. The most talked
about lesbian novel of the nineties!   ISBN 1-56280-030-2   9.95

A DOORYARD FULL OF FLOWERS by Isabel Miller. 160 pp.
Stories incl. 2 sequels to *Patience and Sarah*.   ISBN 1-56280-029-9   9.95

MURDER BY TRADITION by Katherine V. Forrest. 288 pp. A
Kate Delafield Mystery. 4th in a series. ISBN 1-56280-002-7   9.95

THE EROTIC NAIAD edited by Katherine V. Forrest & Barbara Grier.
224 pp. Love stories by Naiad Press authors.   ISBN 1-56280-026-4   12.95

DEAD CERTAIN by Claire McNab. 224 pp. 5th Det. Insp. Carol
Ashton mystery.   ISBN 1-56280-027-2   9.95

CRAZY FOR LOVING by Jaye Maiman. 320 pp. 2nd Robin
Miller mystery.   ISBN 1-56280-025-6   9.95

STONEHURST by Barbara Johnson. 176 pp. Passionate regency
romance.   ISBN 1-56280-024-8   9.95

INTRODUCING AMANDA VALENTINE by Rose Beecham.
256 pp. An Amanda Valentine Mystery — 1st in a series.
ISBN 1-56280-021-3   9.95

UNCERTAIN COMPANIONS by Robbi Sommers. 204 pp.
Steamy, erotic novel.   ISBN 1-56280-017-5   9.95

A TIGER'S HEART by Lauren W. Douglas. 240 pp. Fourth Caitlin
Reece Mystery.   ISBN 1-56280-018-3   9.95

PAPERBACK ROMANCE by Karin Kallmaker. 256 pp. A
delicious romance.   ISBN 1-56280-019-1   9.95

MORTON RIVER VALLEY by Lee Lynch. 304 pp. Lee Lynch at
her best!   ISBN 1-56280-016-7   9.95

THE LAVENDER HOUSE MURDER by Nikki Baker. 224 pp. A
Virginia Kelly Mystery. Second in a series.   ISBN 1-56280-012-4   9.95

PASSION BAY by Jennifer Fulton. 224 pp. Passionate romance,
virgin beaches, tropical skies.   ISBN 1-56280-028-0   9.95

STICKS AND STONES by Jackie Calhoun. 208 pp. Contemporary
lesbian lives and loves.   ISBN 1-56280-020-5   9.95

DELIA IRONFOOT by Jeane Harris. 192 pp. Adventure for Delia
and Beth in the Utah mountains.   ISBN 1-56280-014-0   9.95

UNDER THE SOUTHERN CROSS by Claire McNab. 192 pp.
Romantic nights Down Under.   ISBN 1-56280-011-6   9.95

RIVERFINGER WOMEN by Elana Nachman/Dykewomon.
208 pp. Classic Lesbian/feminist novel. ISBN 1-56280-013-2   8.95

A CERTAIN DISCONTENT by Cleve Boutell. 240 pp. A unique
coterie of women.   ISBN 1-56280-009-4   9.95

GRASSY FLATS by Penny Hayes. 256 pp. Lesbian romance in
the '30s.   ISBN 1-56280-010-8   9.95

A SINGULAR SPY by Amanda K. Williams. 192 pp. 3rd spy novel
featuring Lesbian agent Madison McGuire. ISBN 1-56280-008-6   8.95

THE END OF APRIL by Penny Sumner. 240 pp. A Victoria Cross
Mystery. First in a series.   ISBN 1-56280-007-8   8.95

A FLIGHT OF ANGELS by Sarah Aldridge. 240 pp. Romance set at
the National Gallery of Art   ISBN 1-56280-001-9   9.95

HOUSTON TOWN by Deborah Powell. 208 pp. A Hollis Carpenter
mystery. Second in a series.   ISBN 1-56280-006-X   8.95

KISS AND TELL by Robbi Sommers. 192 pp. Scorching stories by
the author of *Pleasures*.   ISBN 1-56280-005-1   9.95

STILL WATERS by Pat Welch. 208 pp. Second in the Helen
Black mystery series.   ISBN 0-941483-97-5   9.95

MURDER IS GERMANE by Karen Saum. 224 pp. The 2nd
Brigid Donovan mystery.   ISBN 0-941483-98-3   8.95

TO LOVE AGAIN by Evelyn Kennedy. 208 pp. Wildly
romantic love story.   ISBN 0-941483-85-1   9.95

IN THE GAME by Nikki Baker. 192 pp. A Virginia Kelly
mystery. First in a series.   ISBN 01-56280-004-3   9.95

AVALON by Mary Jane Jones. 256 pp. A Lesbian Arthurian
romance.   ISBN 0-941483-96-7   9.95

STRANDED by Camarin Grae. 320 pp. Entertaining, riveting
adventure.   ISBN 0-941483-99-1   9.95

THE DAUGHTERS OF ARTEMIS by Lauren Wright Douglas.
240 pp. Third Caitlin Reece mystery.   ISBN 0-941483-95-9   9.95

CLEARWATER by Catherine Ennis. 176 pp. Romantic secrets
of a small Louisiana town.   ISBN 0-941483-65-7   8.95

THE HALLELUJAH MURDERS by Dorothy Tell. 176 pp.
Second Poppy Dillworth mystery.   ISBN 0-941483-88-6   8.95

ZETA BASE by Judith Alguire. 208 pp. Lesbian triangle
on a future Earth.   ISBN 0-941483-94-0   9.95

SECOND CHANCE by Jackie Calhoun. 256 pp. Contemporary
Lesbian lives and loves.   ISBN 0-941483-93-2   9.95

BENEDICTION by Diane Salvatore. 272 pp. Striking,
contemporary romantic novel.   ISBN 0-941483-90-8   9.95

CALLING RAIN by Karen Marie Christa Minns. 240 pp.
Spellbinding, erotic love story   ISBN 0-941483-87-8   9.95

BLACK IRIS by Jeane Harris. 192 pp. Caroline's hidden past . . .
                                        ISBN 0-941483-68-1   8.95

TOUCHWOOD by Karin Kallmaker. 240 pp. Loving, May/
December romance.   ISBN 0-941483-76-2   9.95

BAYOU CITY SECRETS by Deborah Powell. 224 pp. A Hollis
Carpenter mystery. First in a series.   ISBN 0-941483-91-6   9.95

COP OUT by Claire McNab. 208 pp. 4th Det. Insp. Carol Ashton
mystery.   ISBN 0-941483-84-3   9.95

LODESTAR by Phyllis Horn. 224 pp. Romantic, fast-moving
adventure.   ISBN 0-941483-83-5   8.95

THE BEVERLY MALIBU by Katherine V. Forrest. 288 pp. A
Kate Delafield Mystery. 3rd in a series. ISBN 0-941483-48-7   9.95

THAT OLD STUDEBAKER by Lee Lynch. 272 pp. Andy's affair
with Regina and her attachment to her beloved car.
                                        ISBN 0-941483-82-7   9.95

PASSION'S LEGACY by Lori Paige. 224 pp. Sarah is swept into
the arms of Augusta Pym in this delightful historical romance.
                                        ISBN 0-941483-81-9   8.95

THE PROVIDENCE FILE by Amanda Kyle Williams. 256 pp.
Second espionage thriller featuring lesbian agent Madison McGuire
ISBN 0-941483-92-4   8.95

I LEFT MY HEART by Jaye Maiman. 320 pp. A Robin Miller
Mystery. First in a series.   ISBN 0-941483-72-X   9.95

THE PRICE OF SALT by Patricia Highsmith (writing as Claire
Morgan). 288 pp. Classic lesbian novel, first issued in 1952 . . .
acknowledged by its author under her own, very famous, name.
ISBN 1-56280-003-5   9.95

SIDE BY SIDE by Isabel Miller. 256 pp. From beloved author of
Patience and Sarah.   ISBN 0-941483-77-0   9.95

SOUTHBOUND by Sheila Ortiz Taylor. 240 pp. Hilarious sequel
to *Faultline.*   ISBN 0-941483-78-9   8.95

STAYING POWER: LONG TERM LESBIAN COUPLES
by Susan E. Johnson. 352 pp. Joys of coupledom.
ISBN 0-941-483-75-4   12.95

SLICK by Camarin Grae. 304 pp. Exotic, erotic adventure.
ISBN 0-941483-74-6   9.95

NINTH LIFE by Lauren Wright Douglas. 256 pp. A Caitlin
Reece mystery. 2nd in a series.   ISBN 0-941483-50-9   8.95

PLAYERS by Robbi Sommers. 192 pp. Sizzling, erotic novel.
ISBN 0-941483-73-8   9.95

MURDER AT RED ROOK RANCH by Dorothy Tell. 224 pp.
First Poppy Dillworth adventure.   ISBN 0-941483-80-0   8.95

LESBIAN SURVIVAL MANUAL by Rhonda Dicksion.
112 pp. Cartoons!   ISBN 0-941483-71-1   8.95

A ROOM FULL OF WOMEN by Elisabeth Nonas. 256 pp.
Contemporary Lesbian lives.   ISBN 0-941483-69-X   9.95

MURDER IS RELATIVE by Karen Saum. 256 pp. The first
Brigid Donovan mystery.   ISBN 0-941483-70-3   8.95

PRIORITIES by Lynda Lyons 288 pp. Science fiction with
a twist.   ISBN 0-941483-66-5   8.95

THEME FOR DIVERSE INSTRUMENTS by Jane Rule. 208
pp. Powerful romantic lesbian stories.   ISBN 0-941483-63-0   8.95

LESBIAN QUERIES by Hertz & Ertman. 112 pp. The questions
you were too embarrassed to ask.   ISBN 0-941483-67-3   8.95

CLUB 12 by Amanda Kyle Williams. 288 pp. Espionage thriller
featuring a lesbian agent!   ISBN 0-941483-64-9   8.95

DEATH DOWN UNDER by Claire McNab. 240 pp. 3rd Det.
Insp. Carol Ashton mystery.   ISBN 0-941483-39-8   9.95

MONTANA FEATHERS by Penny Hayes. 256 pp. Vivian and
Elizabeth find love in frontier Montana.   ISBN 0-941483-61-4   8.95

CHESAPEAKE PROJECT by Phyllis Horn. 304 pp. Jessie &
Meredith in perilous adventure.   ISBN 0-941483-58-4   8.95

LIFESTYLES by Jackie Calhoun. 224 pp. Contemporary Lesbian
lives and loves.   ISBN 0-941483-57-6   9.95

VIRAGO by Karen Marie Christa Minns. 208 pp. Darsen has
chosen Ginny.   ISBN 0-941483-56-8   8.95

WILDERNESS TREK by Dorothy Tell. 192 pp. Six women on
vacation learning "new" skills.   ISBN 0-941483-60-6   8.95

MURDER BY THE BOOK by Pat Welch. 256 pp. A Helen
Black Mystery. First in a series.   ISBN 0-941483-59-2   9.95

BERRIGAN by Vicki P. McConnell. 176 pp. Youthful Lesbian —
romantic, idealistic Berrigan.   ISBN 0-941483-55-X   8.95

LESBIANS IN GERMANY by Lillian Faderman & B. Eriksson.
128 pp. Fiction, poetry, essays.   ISBN 0-941483-62-2   8.95

THERE'S SOMETHING I'VE BEEN MEANING TO TELL
YOU Ed. by Loralee MacPike. 288 pp. Gay men and lesbians
coming out to their children.   ISBN 0-941483-44-4   9.95

LIFTING BELLY by Gertrude Stein. Ed. by Rebecca Mark. 104
pp. Erotic poetry.   ISBN 0-941483-51-7   8.95

ROSE PENSKI by Roz Perry. 192 pp. Adult lovers in a long-term
relationship.   ISBN 0-941483-37-1   8.95

AFTER THE FIRE by Jane Rule. 256 pp. Warm, human novel
by this incomparable author.   ISBN 0-941483-45-2   8.95

SUE SLATE, PRIVATE EYE by Lee Lynch. 176 pp. The gay
folk of Peacock Alley are *all cats*.   ISBN 0-941483-52-5   8.95

CHRIS by Randy Salem. 224 pp. Golden oldie. Handsome Chris
and her adventures.   ISBN 0-941483-42-8   8.95

THREE WOMEN by March Hastings. 232 pp. Golden oldie. A
triangle among wealthy sophisticates.   ISBN 0-941483-43-6   8.95

RICE AND BEANS by Valeria Taylor. 232 pp. Love and
romance on poverty row.   ISBN 0-941483-41-X   8.95

PLEASURES by Robbi Sommers. 204 pp. Unprecedented
eroticism.   ISBN 0-941483-49-5   8.95

EDGEWISE by Camarin Grae. 372 pp. Spellbinding
adventure.   ISBN 0-941483-19-3   9.95

FATAL REUNION by Claire McNab. 224 pp. 2nd Det. Inspec.
Carol Ashton mystery.   ISBN 0-941483-40-1   8.95

KEEP TO ME STRANGER by Sarah Aldridge. 372 pp. Romance
set in a department store dynasty.   ISBN 0-941483-38-X   9.95

HEARTSCAPE by Sue Gambill. 204 pp. American lesbian in
Portugal.   ISBN 0-941483-33-9   8.95

IN THE BLOOD by Lauren Wright Douglas. 252 pp. Lesbian
science fiction adventure fantasy   ISBN 0-941483-22-3   8.95

THE BEE'S KISS by Shirley Verel. 216 pp. Delicate, delicious
romance.   ISBN 0-941483-36-3   8.95

RAGING MOTHER MOUNTAIN by Pat Emmerson. 264 pp.
Furosa Firechild's adventures in Wonderland.   ISBN 0-941483-35-5   8.95

IN EVERY PORT by Karin Kallmaker. 228 pp. Jessica's sexy,
adventuresome travels.   ISBN 0-941483-37-7   9.95

OF LOVE AND GLORY by Evelyn Kennedy. 192 pp. Exciting
WWII romance.   ISBN 0-941483-32-0   8.95

CLICKING STONES by Nancy Tyler Glenn. 288 pp. Love
transcending time.   ISBN 0-941483-31-2   9.95

SURVIVING SISTERS by Gail Pass. 252 pp. Powerful love
story.   ISBN 0-941483-16-9   8.95

SOUTH OF THE LINE by Catherine Ennis. 216 pp. Civil War
adventure.   ISBN 0-941483-29-0   8.95

WOMAN PLUS WOMAN by Dolores Klaich. 300 pp. Supurb
Lesbian overview.   ISBN 0-941483-28-2   9.95

SLOW DANCING AT MISS POLLY'S by Sheila Ortiz Taylor.
96 pp. Lesbian Poetry   ISBN 0-941483-30-4   7.95

DOUBLE DAUGHTER by Vicki P. McConnell. 216 pp. A Nyla
Wade Mystery, third in the series.   ISBN 0-941483-26-6   8.95

HEAVY GILT by Delores Klaich. 192 pp. Lesbian detective/
disappearing homophobes/upper class gay society.

ISBN 0-941483-25-8   8.95

THE FINER GRAIN by Denise Ohio. 216 pp. Brilliant young
college lesbian novel.   ISBN 0-941483-11-8   8.95

THE AMAZON TRAIL by Lee Lynch. 216 pp. Life, travel & lore
of famous lesbian author.   ISBN 0-941483-27-4   8.95

HIGH CONTRAST by Jessie Lattimore. 264 pp. Women of the
Crystal Palace.   ISBN 0-941483-17-7   8.95

OCTOBER OBSESSION by Meredith More. Josie's rich, secret
Lesbian life.   ISBN 0-941483-18-5   8.95

LESBIAN CROSSROADS by Ruth Baetz. 276 pp. Contemporary
Lesbian lives.   ISBN 0-941483-21-5   9.95

BEFORE STONEWALL: THE MAKING OF A GAY AND
LESBIAN COMMUNITY by Andrea Weiss & Greta Schiller.
96 pp., 25 illus.   ISBN 0-941483-20-7   7.95

WE WALK THE BACK OF THE TIGER by Patricia A. Murphy.
192 pp. Romantic Lesbian novel/beginning women's movement.

ISBN 0-941483-13-4   8.95

SUNDAY'S CHILD by Joyce Bright. 216 pp. Lesbian athletics, at
last the novel about sports.   ISBN 0-941483-12-6   8.95

OSTEN'S BAY by Zenobia N. Vole. 204 pp. Sizzling adventure
romance set on Bonaire.   ISBN 0-941483-15-0   8.95

LESSONS IN MURDER by Claire McNab. 216 pp. 1st Det. Inspec.
Carol Ashton mystery — erotic tension!.   ISBN 0-941483-14-2   8.95

YELLOWTHROAT by Penny Hayes. 240 pp. Margarita, bandit,
kidnaps Julia.   ISBN 0-941483-10-X   8.95

SAPPHISTRY: THE BOOK OF LESBIAN SEXUALITY by
Pat Califia. 3d edition, revised. 208 pp.   ISBN 0-941483-24-X   10.95

CHERISHED LOVE by Evelyn Kennedy. 192 pp. Erotic
Lesbian love story.   ISBN 0-941483-08-8   9.95

LAST SEPTEMBER by Helen R. Hull. 208 pp. Six stories & a
glorious novella.   ISBN 0-941483-09-6   8.95

THE SECRET IN THE BIRD by Camarin Grae. 312 pp. Striking,
psychological suspense novel.   ISBN 0-941483-05-3   8.95

TO THE LIGHTNING by Catherine Ennis. 208 pp. Romantic
Lesbian 'Robinson Crusoe' adventure.   ISBN 0-941483-06-1   8.95

THE OTHER SIDE OF VENUS by Shirley Verel. 224 pp.
Luminous, romantic love story.   ISBN 0-941483-07-X   8.95

DREAMS AND SWORDS by Katherine V. Forrest. 192 pp.
Romantic, erotic, imaginative stories.   ISBN 0-941483-03-7   8.95

MEMORY BOARD by Jane Rule. 336 pp. Memorable novel
about an aging Lesbian couple.   ISBN 0-941483-02-9   9.95

THE ALWAYS ANONYMOUS BEAST by Lauren Wright
Douglas. 224 pp. A Caitlin Reece mystery. First in a series.
                                          ISBN 0-941483-04-5   8.95

SEARCHING FOR SPRING by Patricia A. Murphy. 224 pp.
Novel about the recovery of love.   ISBN 0-941483-00-2   8.95

DUSTY'S QUEEN OF HEARTS DINER by Lee Lynch. 240 pp.
Romantic blue-collar novel.   ISBN 0-941483-01-0   8.95

PARENTS MATTER by Ann Muller. 240 pp. Parents'
relationships with Lesbian daughters and gay sons.
                                          ISBN 0-930044-91-6   9.95

THE PEARLS by Shelley Smith. 176 pp. Passion and fun in
the Caribbean sun.   ISBN 0-930044-93-2   7.95

MAGDALENA by Sarah Aldridge. 352 pp. Epic Lesbian novel
set on three continents.   ISBN 0-930044-99-1   8.95

THE BLACK AND WHITE OF IT by Ann Allen Shockley.
144 pp. Short stories.   ISBN 0-930044-96-7   7.95

SAY JESUS AND COME TO ME by Ann Allen Shockley. 288
pp. Contemporary romance.   ISBN 0-930044-98-3   8.95

LOVING HER by Ann Allen Shockley. 192 pp. Romantic love
story.   ISBN 0-930044-97-5   7.95

MURDER AT THE NIGHTWOOD BAR by Katherine V.
Forrest. 240 pp. A Kate Delafield mystery. Second in a series.
                                      ISBN 0-930044-92-4   9.95

ZOE'S BOOK by Gail Pass. 224 pp. Passionate, obsessive love
story.   ISBN 0-930044-95-9   7.95

WINGED DANCER by Camarin Grae. 228 pp. Erotic Lesbian
adventure story.   ISBN 0-930044-88-6   8.95

PAZ by Camarin Grae. 336 pp. Romantic Lesbian adventurer
with the power to change the world.   ISBN 0-930044-89-4   8.95

SOUL SNATCHER by Camarin Grae. 224 pp. A puzzle, an
adventure, a mystery — Lesbian romance.   ISBN 0-930044-90-8   8.95

THE LOVE OF GOOD WOMEN by Isabel Miller. 224 pp.
Long-awaited new novel by the author of the beloved *Patience
and Sarah.*   ISBN 0-930044-81-9   8.95

THE HOUSE AT PELHAM FALLS by Brenda Weathers. 240
pp. Suspenseful Lesbian ghost story. ISBN 0-930044-79-7   7.95

HOME IN YOUR HANDS by Lee Lynch. 240 pp. More stories
from the author of *Old Dyke Tales.* ISBN 0-930044-80-0   7.95

EACH HAND A MAP by Anita Skeen. 112 pp. Real-life poems
that touch us all.   ISBN 0-930044-82-7   6.95

SURPLUS by Sylvia Stevenson. 342 pp. A classic early Lesbian
novel.   ISBN 0-930044-78-9   7.95

PEMBROKE PARK by Michelle Martin. 256 pp. Derring-do
and daring romance in Regency England.   ISBN 0-930044-77-0   7.95

THE LONG TRAIL by Penny Hayes. 248 pp. Vivid adventures
of two women in love in the old west.   ISBN 0-930044-76-2   8.95

HORIZON OF THE HEART by Shelley Smith. 192 pp. Hot
romance in summertime New England.   ISBN 0-930044-75-4   7.95

AN EMERGENCE OF GREEN by Katherine V. Forrest. 288
pp. Powerful novel of sexual discovery.   ISBN 0-930044-69-X   9.95

THE LESBIAN PERIODICALS INDEX edited by Claire
Potter. 432 pp. Author & subject index.   ISBN 0-930044-74-6   29.95

DESERT OF THE HEART by Jane Rule. 224 pp. A classic;
basis for the movie *Desert Hearts.* ISBN 0-930044-73-8   9.95

SPRING FORWARD/FALL BACK by Sheila Ortiz Taylor.
288 pp. Literary novel of timeless love.   ISBN 0-930044-70-3   7.95

FOR KEEPS by Elisabeth Nonas. 144 pp. Contemporary novel
about losing and finding love.   ISBN 0-930044-71-1   7.95

TORCHLIGHT TO VALHALLA by Gale Wilhelm. 128 pp.
Classic novel by a great Lesbian writer.   ISBN 0-930044-68-1   7.95

TO THE CLEVELAND STATION by Carol Anne Douglas.
192 pp. Interracial Lesbian love story. ISBN 0-930044-27-4 6.95

THE NESTING PLACE by Sarah Aldridge. 224 pp. A
three-woman triangle — love conquers all! ISBN 0-930044-26-6 7.95

THIS IS NOT FOR YOU by Jane Rule. 284 pp. A letter to a
beloved is also an intricate novel. ISBN 0-930044-25-8 8.95

FAULTLINE by Sheila Ortiz Taylor. 140 pp. Warm, funny,
literate story of a startling family. ISBN 0-930044-24-X 6.95

ANNA'S COUNTRY by Elizabeth Lang. 208 pp. A woman
finds her Lesbian identity. ISBN 0-930044-19-3 8.95

PRISM by Valerie Taylor. 158 pp. A love affair between two
women in their sixties. ISBN 0-930044-18-5 6.95

OUTLANDER by Jane Rule. 207 pp. Short stories and essays
by one of our finest writers. ISBN 0-930044-17-7 8.95

ALL TRUE LOVERS by Sarah Aldridge. 292 pp. Romantic
novel set in the 1930s and 1940s. ISBN 0-930044-10-X 8.95

A WOMAN APPEARED TO ME by Renee Vivien. 65 pp. A
classic; translated by Jeannette H. Foster. ISBN 0-930044-06-1 5.00

CYTHEREA'S BREATH by Sarah Aldridge. 240 pp. Romantic
novel about women's entrance into medicine.
 ISBN 0-930044-02-9 6.95

TOTTIE by Sarah Aldridge. 181 pp. Lesbian romance in the
turmoil of the sixties. ISBN 0-930044-01-0 6.95

THE LATECOMER by Sarah Aldridge. 107 pp. A delicate love
story. ISBN 0-930044-00-2 6.95

ODD GIRL OUT by Ann Bannon. ISBN 0-930044-83-5 5.95
I AM A WOMAN 84-3; WOMEN IN THE SHADOWS 85-1; each
JOURNEY TO A WOMAN 86-X; BEEBO BRINKER 87-8. Golden
oldies about life in Greenwich Village.

JOURNEY TO FULFILLMENT, A WORLD WITHOUT MEN, and 3.95
RETURN TO LESBOS. All by Valerie Taylor each

These are just a few of the many Naiad Press titles — we are the oldest and
largest lesbian/feminist publishing company in the world. Please request a
complete catalog. We offer personal service; we encourage and welcome direct
mail orders from individuals who have limited access to bookstores carrying
our publications.